*"Perhaps I should stay and make sure
you don't have any trouble getting in
and out of the tub? I promise to keep
my eyes closed."*

Rosalyn would have preferred that Derek join her in the warm, silky water, and the thought danced through her head of whispering an indecent invitation. "Thank you, but I'm sure I'll be fine."

A roguish grin lifted his lips. "Do you realize how much time we spend thanking each other?"

Rosalyn couldn't help a smile of her own. "Quite a bit, I believe."

"One might think we're avoiding something else."

"Like what?" But she knew. The sexual connection between them had been flame-hot from the start.

"I can think of any number of things, none of which I feel inclined to discuss just now," he replied in a husky tone.

Rosalyn's heart skipped a beat at the look in Derek's eyes, and her breathing grew shallow as he drew nearer. "Perhaps I should take my bath."

He wrapped an arm around her waist and pulled her tight against his chest. "I know I said I wouldn't do this again," he murmured against her lips, "but I can't seem to help myself."

"Derek," she moaned, knowing with utterance what she was asking f

Acclaim for
THE ART OF SEDUCTION

"The sex scenes are great, the secondary characters interesting, and the resolution satisfying." —*Booklist*

"The delightful characters, sensual and fun plot, and witty dialogue are all hallmarks of Ms. George's charming romances." —*Romantic Times*

. . . and praise for her previous national bestselling fiction

"[A]n expert storyteller. . . . [A] memorable, fast-paced tale that puts Melanie George on your must-read list!" —*Romantic Times*

"It's a winner, with one of romance's feistiest heroines and most alluringly brooding heroes." —*Booklist*

"Melanie George writes hot, steamy historicals with characters that leap off the page with spunk and spitfire." —*Bridges Magazine*

"A treasure, a triumph, a treat for the heart! [T]ender, witty, and utterly charming. . . . Ms. George just keeps getting better and better." —*Old Book Barn Gazette*

"[P]aradise found!" —*Midwest Book Review*

"Sparkling wit and charming characters." —*Affaire de Coeur*

The Highlander's Stolen Bride

MELANIE GEORGE

POCKET BOOKS

New York   London   Toronto   Sydney

An *Original* Publication of POCKET BOOKS

 POCKET BOOKS, a division of Simon & Schuster, Inc.
1230 Avenue of the Americas, New York, NY 10020

This book is a work of fiction. Names, characters, places, and incidents are products of the author's imagination or are used fictitiously. Any resemblance to actual events or locales or persons, living or dead, is entirely coincidental.

Copyright © 2006 by Melanie George

ISBN-13: 978-0-7434-4275-6
ISBN-10:   0-7434-4275-X

First Pocket Books printing February 2006

10 9 8 7 6 5 4 3 2 1

POCKET and colophon are registered trademarks of Simon & Schuster, Inc.

Front cover illustration by Franco Accornero

Manufactured in the United States of America

For information regarding special discounts for bulk purchases, please contact Simon & Schuster Special Sales at 1-800-456-6798 or business@simonandschuster.com.

As always, much love to my wonderful readers.
Thank you for your unfailing support and praise.

The Highlander's Stolen Bride

One

Rosalyn had the dream again.

It was the same dream she had been having for years, but the ending would always fade, leaving her flushed and breathless.

Now *he* had become a part of the dream.

The faces had become theirs, the passion a scorching flame that would heat her skin and have her waking with her nightclothes clinging to her.

She was a woman with secret desires—a woman with an acute sensual instinct, living her private fantasies in the darkest part of the night, in the deepest recesses of her mind, where she could be brazen and audacious.

She had been sixteen the day sexuality awoke inside her untutored body. She had been attending a soiree with her parents. She had gotten lost in the enormous mansion and found herself at the opposite end of the house. She heard a noise behind a closed door, and thought she would find someone there to help her.

She knocked upon the door, but the noises within had only grown louder. She feared the woman she heard crying was in trouble, injured perhaps.

Rosalyn opened the door, and stumbled upon something devastatingly arousing to her senses.

A woman, wearing only a maid's apron around her waist, was down on her knees in front of a tall, fiercely built man with nary a stitch of clothes on. The woman's golden hair cascaded unbound down her back and was clasped in the man's meaty hand as he guided her head forward.

Rosalyn could barely contain her shocked gasp as his thick, hard rod disappeared inch by inch into the woman's mouth, her wet lips clasping and sucking the silky head.

The man's head was tipped back, his lips parted, his breath releasing in a groaning hiss as his stiff member stroked in and out of the woman's mouth, her hands guiding it, savoring it.

He shoved her hands away and pushed forward so the whole of his staff was covered by her moist lips, his movements becoming increasingly frenetic until a moan spilled from his lips, and a white froth erupted from the tip of his member.

Rosalyn stood in shock, unable to move. She must have made a sound, because the man shot a glance toward the door. No look of anger crossed his face. Instead, he smiled, as though pleased to have been caught in such a lascivious act.

"You like what you saw, young one?" he asked in a deep rasp. "Come back to me when the throbbing between your legs needs appeasing. Big John will pleasure you." He grasped the chin of the female still on her knees before him and said, "Won't I, my dear?"

The woman looked at Rosalyn with a cocked eyebrow and a wicked grin. "Oh, yes, he certainly will."

Their laughter followed Rosalyn as she raced down the hallway, stopping only when she ran out of breath. She felt scared—and yet her breasts tingled, and a strange moistness had accumulated in her nether region.

Since that day, Lady Rosalyn Carmichael had used her dreams as a tool as she waited for him—the one. The only man she would grant her virginity.

And as the night wore on toward the morning, her dreams focused on *that* man. A man who had walked out of her dreams and into her real life.

He had eyes of velvet blue, piercing and intense. Black hair glossy as a raven's wing. A body of rugged elegance, brawny beneath his tailored exterior. His beauty mocked all those around him as he smiled at her in a faintly wicked way from across the ballroom.

Rosalyn shivered as he approached, unable to pull her admiring gaze from his tall form, noting how he moved with careless grace, leaving her slightly dazed and barely aware of her best friend, Francine Fitz Hugh, who stood beside her.

Fancy's guardian, Lucien Kendall, walked alongside the darkly beautiful man. When the stranger stopped before Rosalyn and spoke, his deep, low voice tripping along her nerves in the most disconcerting fashion, she knew.

She was doomed.

Rosalyn could read her downfall in the assessing glance he leveled on her, as though he knew a secret he had no intention of telling.

"Derek," she murmured in her sleep, tossing fitfully, reliving the kiss he had given her in Lady Senhaven's garden. The scent of honeysuckle had surrounded them, the guests no more than forty yards away, a scandal in the making as she allowed—nay, begged—him to take liberties, moving his warm, large hand from her waist to her breast, tugging down the material to free the soft globes from their strict confines, loving the way he thumbed her nipples, rolling them lightly, leaving them swollen and sweetly sore as she guided his mouth to them.

A strange sense of abandonment swept over her, an excitement beyond all self-restraint as she placed her hand for the first time against a man's hardness. She felt it lengthen as she caressed it, marveling at its ever-increasing size and at her own power as a woman.

If only the refined people dancing in the ballroom knew that she was not the girl they had labeled an innocent, gently bred and nurtured, elegant, graceful. A proper young woman.

Rosalyn was afraid to let even her best friend,

Fancy, know of that darker side of her nature. Fancy had never judged her, but Rosalyn worried that her friend would look at her differently if she knew the wanton woman she truly was.

The dream suddenly evaporated and her eyes snapped open as a hand clamped down over her mouth, her gasp muffled into a callused palm.

"Utter a single word," a foul-smelling voice hissed, "and y'll be one very sorry miss."

A stranger stood beside her bed, dressed in dark, filthy clothes, the left side of his face obscured by shadows.

"Get up. An' be quiet. There's a man waitin' most impatiently for y'."

Rosalyn was jerked to her bare feet, feeling exposed and frightened in only her nightgown.

Calder had found her!

She had known her stepbrother had not given up in his pursuit, trailing her from Cornwall to London after his unsuccessful attempt at kidnapping her from Moor's End, Fancy's home in Cornwall. Rosalyn had been staying there since learning of Calder's twisted plot to marry her and do away with her, so that he could obtain her inheritance.

The last time he had attempted to accost her, she had put up a fight. This time she would go quietly—she could not jeopardize the people she cared for. Fancy had nearly gotten killed trying to protect her from Calder's last assault; she had to face the swine alone this time.

Rosalyn straightened her spine as the man pushed her toward the window. She swallowed back her fear as she looked down from her room on the second story to the ground below, where a hemp rope swayed unsteadily in the night breeze.

"Make a peep," her kidnapper growled, "an' I'll gut y' like a fish. Now through the window with ye." He gave her a shove.

Rosalyn stumbled forward, her mind working feverishly. If only she was more like Fancy, who had disarmed the two thugs Rosalyn's stepbrother had hired to bring her back to Westcott Manor.

"Out the window," her kidnapper demanded, his tone brooking no argument.

"May I at least get some shoes?" Rosalyn asked, glancing down at her bare feet.

"No," he snapped. "Now get movin'—or do y' want me to toss you over my shoulder an' carry y' down?"

She'd rather fling herself bodily from the roof. "I'll manage, thank you."

Hoisting up the hem of her nightgown, she straddled the windowsill, fervently wishing a white knight would suddenly appear to save her.

Where was Derek right now? Still at the Duvalls' cotillion, flirting with Lady Jane Windermere? "I don't need him anyway," she muttered.

"What's that?" her kidnapper snapped.

Rosalyn dearly yearned to erase his scowl with a bracing punch to his already crooked nose, but she'd probably only succeed in falling out the window.

"Are you sure this ladder will hold? Perhaps we should go by way of the front door."

"Missy," he said, pressing his face close to hers, his breath rank enough to make a skunk turn tail, "y're wearing mightily on my patience, and that ain't a good thing."

With that warning ringing in her ears, Rosalyn tested her right foot on the first rung, then swung her left leg over. She'd make a run for it the moment her feet hit the ground. She could easily outdistance the brute, as he was rather stocky and clearly in less than perfect physical condition.

Her left foot had just settled onto the rung when her bedroom door flew open. A figure loomed on the threshold, backlit by the flickering sconce in the hallway, creating a menacing apparition.

The glint of steel told her a gun was trained in their direction. "Step away from the lady," the voice said, "or I'll blow your bloody head off."

Derek! How had he—

The thug lunged toward the window, causing Rosalyn to swing back, her feet slipping from the rung. She cried out as she began to fall, scrambling for the rope ladder and dangling by a single hand.

Derek's arm thrust through the open window to grab her with one hand. "Hold on," he told her as he struggled with the man, who cried out a moment later as he fell past her and hit the ground with a bone-cracking thud.

Rosalyn stared down at his unmoving form, her fingers twisted painfully in the rope, sheer will all that kept her from the same fate. Derek's hand clamped around her other wrist. "I've got you."

The next moment she was hoisted through the window and clasped tightly in Derek's arms. She fell against his chest and closed her eyes, her whole body trembling.

After a few moments, Derek gently shifted away from her to look down into her eyes, concern etched plainly on his face. "Are you hurt?" he asked.

"Dear heavens, what's going on here?" a voice called out.

Rosalyn glanced over Derek's shoulder to find Lady Dane standing in the doorway, her long mahogany hair unbound and flowing around her shoulders, her wrapper trailing behind her, confirming that she had flung herself from bed.

"An intruder made his way into her bedroom," Derek explained.

"Sweet Lord." Clarisse hastened into the room and knelt down beside Rosalyn.

"I'm all right," Rosalyn assured her.

"Come, my dear," Clarisse gently urged, patting Rosalyn's hand. "Let's get you to the bed."

Derek lifted Rosalyn into his arms, ignoring her protests. Once she was settled, he said, "I'll check the grounds and send for the constable."

"Thank you," Clarisse said as Derek headed out of the room, his face a mask of deadly seriousness. Rosalyn almost felt sorry for whomever he might run across.

How she wished she had never let Fancy talk her into coming to London! She had only managed to involve yet another person in Calder's evil intentions.

"I'm sorry," she said. "I didn't mean for any of us this to happen. I'll leave in the morning."

Clarisse waved a dismissive hand. "Nonsense, you're not going anywhere. If you think I'll allow a mere cretin to scare me, you have much to learn." As though Rosalyn were a child in need of care, her hostess adjusted the pillows behind her head.

"I should go home," Rosalyn insisted, knowing that nothing awaited her there. Her parents were both gone, and the man who had treated her like a daughter for five years had succumbed to illness a few weeks earlier, leaving Rosalyn with no one but a stepbrother who wished her dead.

"Home?" Clarisse scoffed. "That's out of the question. Think rationally, my dear. This is the best place for you. Derek is a champion pugilist. He won't let anything happen to you. Nor will I."

"But if anything were to happen to you . . ."

"Nothing will happen to me. Besides, I could use a bit of excitement in my life. Now, I assume this was the work of your diabolical stepbrother?"

Rosalyn nodded. "I don't know how he found me. Mr. Kendall was so cautious with my safety."

"I'm sure he was. But desperate men will go to desperate measures. The only way we shall put an end to his machinations is to catch him."

"Calder is slippery. He always stays one step ahead."

"Then we need someone who shall stay two steps ahead. Someone far more dangerous and ruthless than Calder will ever be."

Derek regarded himself in the mirror above the mantel in Clarisse's plush living room and saw a man who had aged ten years in a matter of minutes.

An hour ago he had left the Duvalls' soiree, unable to endure the mindless chatter of his on-again off-again paramour, Lady Jane Windermere.

There was a time not long ago when he would have tolerated the woman's endless rambling about herself, knowing that once he had her in bed, moans rather than blather would pour from her lips.

But he had noticed something disturbing: a growing boredom with the opposite sex. And he was a man of enormous carnal appetites, which had earned him a place in an exclusive bachelor's club, the Pleasure Seekers. The other six members were his closest friends in the world, whom he would trust with his very life, and vice versa.

Yet his restlessness went deeper, to a level he didn't want to examine. A need had begun to stir within him, a desire to do something no devout bachelor would ever do.

Settle down with one woman.

He envisioned eyes of green fire and hair of the palest blond that fell nearly waist-length, like some fair maiden from a book of yore. But Lady Rosalyn Carmichael was very real.

She had caught his eye the moment she had entered Clarisse's ballroom three weeks ago for the coming-out ball of Lucien's ward, Lady Francine. Derek had never believed in angels, or God for that matter, but the sight of Rosalyn had made him a believer. Only a higher power could have created something so exceptionally lovely.

But it was far more than her beauty that drew him to her; it was the hint of sadness and vulnerability he glimpsed in her eyes. He had felt a strong desire to protect her—even before Lucien had filled him in on the girl's murderous stepbrother, Calder Westcott, a man Derek's fists longed to meet.

Derek stared at the rope that he had yanked down from Rosalyn's bedroom window. If he had been any later . . . He didn't want to contemplate what would have happened.

He wondered how Rosalyn was faring at that moment. Was she still frightened? Did she need him? He desperately wanted to go check on her, make sure she was all right. He'd nearly had a heart attack when he saw a shapely leg swing over the side of the windowsill, and then spotted the flaxen hair he had imagined gathering into his hands all night.

Derek didn't know what had drawn him to her doorstep. He hadn't consciously decided to go to Clarisse's house after leaving the soiree, but that was where his feet had taken him.

Behind him, the door to the parlor quietly opened, then closed. "I see you've availed yourself of the liquor."

Derek turned and watched Clarisse as she moved

with subtle grace across the floor. She was still a spectacular-looking woman, and many men would have killed to have her, but since her husband's death she had chosen to remain alone. She was a strong woman, and he admired her. He was glad they had remained friends all these years.

"Mind pouring me one?" she asked.

"Already did," he replied, reaching behind him for her glass.

"You always were a resourceful man."

Derek nodded toward the door. "How is she?"

"She claims to be perfectly fine. but while she is a surprisingly strong young woman, considering what's she's been through, I doubt she's fine at all. She does not want to burden anyone, which only adds to her struggle. She could use a protector, and quickly."

"Are you suggesting I assume that role?"

Clarisse smiled demurely over the rim of her glass. "I'm suggesting no such thing, my lord."

Derek shook his head. "You always were a cagey woman, Lady Dane. Far too smart for the likes of the men who pursue you so vigorously."

Clarisse sighed and sat down on the settee. "I fear she will try to leave."

Derek had worried about the same thing. "Where might she go?"

Clarisse shrugged. "I don't know. She's got no one. Her horrid brother appears to be the only family she has left. How terrible to have to live in fear of the people who should protect and cherish you.

"Well," she continued with a sigh, "I shall come up with something. You've done more than your share. Had you not arrived when you did . . ." She shivered, then cocked her head and frowned. "Why, exactly, were you here in the middle of the night?"

"I was restless, so I went for a stroll."

"A stroll, hmm?" A slight grin turned up the corners of Clarisse's lips. "How very fortuitous for us."

Derek glared. "Yes."

"Well," she sighed, rising to her feet, "I must get back to check on my guest. And you must get home. If I remember correctly, you are leaving tomorrow for Scotland."

"Yes." He had come to England only to settle his mother's estate. Now that that had been taken care of, he had no reason to stay.

Except for Rosalyn.

Something about her pulled at him. He had never considered himself particularly heroic, although Megan, the lass he had grown up with, would disagree. Her five very protective older brothers, however, did not share her opinion. They believed he should be skinned and hung from his ankles.

"Are you all right?" Clarisse asked, regarding him with a furrowed brow.

"Fine." He stared down into his drink. "I'd like to stay on your couch tonight, make sure nothing else happens." When he glanced up, he found Clarisse smiling again.

"That would be wonderful. I'd feel ever so much safer knowing you're here—as would Rosalyn," she added pointedly. "I would prefer you sleep in a real bed, however, since I have seven of them. Perhaps the room next to Lady Rosalyn's?"

The temptation would be great, but what would be his excuse for declining? "That will be fine. Thank you."

Derek followed Clarisse from the room, telling himself that he was just staying until the morning to make sure nothing more transpired during the night and to see that Rosalyn had sufficiently recovered from her experience. Once he knew she was safe and taken care of, he would depart.

He would hire a protector for her. A Pinkerton man, perhaps. He also knew a high-ranking constable who had recently gone into business for himself, a fine fellow with spotless credentials. Either one would do.

Derek glanced at Rosalyn's closed bedroom door as Clarisse opened the next door over and gestured him inside. As he bid her good night, he wondered why he didn't feel the least bit pleased with his decision.

Two

Rosalyn sat bolt upright, her eyes snapping open as a scream built in her throat. She glanced wildly around the bedroom, certain a hand had been covering her mouth, and that hot, foul breath had fanned her neck. But she was utterly alone—the only thing that had touched her was the morning sunlight spilling through the curtains. It had been a bad dream.

Daybreak had finally arrived, but she had slept only sporadically, her mind whirring with thoughts of what had nearly happened the night before. Something had to be done about her predicament. And now.

She had not allowed herself to believe how far her stepbrother would go, but she now knew how determined Calder was. He wouldn't give up until he had her where he wanted her.

Wed.

And dead.

Rosalyn rose from the bed. Never had she felt more alone than she did at that moment. She paced the length of her room and stopped at the window to look out at the already bustling street below. London, with all its mysteries and delights, had been a welcome surprise, making Cornwall seem as though it existed in another time and place.

An idea began to form in Rosalyn's head. Surely she could get lost in a city of this magnitude. Why, there had to be endless places a young woman could hide! That could work. It must.

Refusing to listen to the little voice that reminded her that a lady of breeding did not travel alone, she decided to view this as an adventure. A tale of derring-do that she could relate to little children on cold winter nights.

She dropped down onto the edge of the bed with a sigh. There would be no children of her own to tell her tales to. She was barren. Infertile.

A raging childhood case of scarlet fever meant there would never be a little boy or girl to call her own. But this was not the time to wallow in self-pity; she needed to come up with a plan.

Calder had another thing coming if he expected her to be a lamb heading to his slaughter; this was a fight she intended to win.

Hastening into her morning dress, Rosalyn dragged her trunk out of the closet, swiftly tossing in her clothes with none of the care that had gone into the original packing. She frowned when the top would not close.

"Drat." She plunked down on the lid and bounced, to no avail. She glared at the trunk, confounded.

"Well," she sighed, "the chiffon ball gown will have to go. I'll have no need for it anyway."

Throwing the lid open, Rosalyn tossed the costly evening dress over her shoulder, pleased with the space she had achieved.

With a hop, she resumed her position, but the lid still resisted her efforts. Huffing, she shifted to her knees and bent over the trunk, her rear end in the air and her hair hanging in her face as she fiddled with the lock.

When the bedroom door swung open, it startled her so much that she lost her precarious balance and toppled to the floor, yards of delicate ruffles and lace nearly smothering her.

Spitting out a ribbon that had found its way into her mouth, Rosalyn prepared to give the housemaid a piece of her mind. But all thoughts of anger vanished as mortification took its place. For staring down at her was the last person she wished to see her with her skirt bunched up around her neck and her pantalets exposed.

Lord, her skirt!

Rosalyn lurched upright and wrenched the unruly material down as embarrassment burned from her cheeks all the way to her toes, leaving her staring dumbly at perfectly buffed Hessians that would undoubtedly reveal the extent of her humiliation were she to look into their mirror-like shine.

She didn't know which was worse—nearly being kidnapped, or being found arse-up on the floor by the most stunning man the Lord had put upon the earth.

"My lady?" Derek's outstretched hand appeared in Rosalyn's line of vision, and her first impulse was to slap it away. Had the rude creature seen fit to knock, she would not be in her current state.

With as much dignity as she could muster, she rose to her feet. When Rosalyn met Lord Manchester's bluer-than-blue eyes, she nearly forgot what it was she had intended to say. It was not normal to be so infatuated. He was just a man—he behaved as others of his gender did, spoke in the same cultured tones, could wear no more than a single pair of trousers at any given time, and did not possess any special qualities that she could discern. And yet . . .

He was not like any other man she had ever encountered. He was the one who could fulfill her fantasies, bring to life the hot, sultry dreams that tormented her night after restless night.

"Forgive my unpardonable breach of etiquette, my lady," he said, though his tone and manner implied he would barge in on her again if it suited him to do so. "I fear I couldn't contain my concern for your safety."

Rosalyn lifted her chin. "My safety? How ironic, considering you nearly gave me apoplexy with your unannounced arrival."

"Please accept my apologies. I heard several loud thuds as I was dressing."

"Dressing?" Rosalyn frowned. Why would he be dressing? Then a terrible thought struck her. Had he slept with Lady Dane? Clarisse was a beautiful woman. Men adored her. Perhaps Derek did, as well.

"Yes, I stayed the night. I was in the next room."

Clarisse's bedroom was at the end of the hall. "Why?" she asked.

"I wanted to make sure your slumber remained peaceful." His voice held an odd warmth.

Rosalyn blinked. "Oh." Oh, indeed. He had stayed for her. It was almost unbearably sweet, and she felt the strangest desire to reach up and kiss his cheek. She had to turn from him to put a safe distance between them.

Had he heard her tossing and turning all night? What if she had run screaming from her bed and ran smack into him garbed in nothing but her nightgown? Would he think her mad?

Or would he hold her close and whisper calming words in her ear? Somehow she knew he would. She would melt, undoubtedly, and then act out her desires, tug him back into her room by the lapels of his shirt and drag him down to the bed on top of her. He would sprinkle warm kisses down her neck as his hand traveled up her calf, over her thigh, and between her legs. And oh . . . yes, he would touch her there, skim a single finger along the moist seam and part her, touch her engorged peak, working her effortlessly toward ecstasy.

"Are you all right, my lady?"

Derek's voice yanked Rosalyn back to the present. She turned abruptly from him, her cheeks scarlet. "Perfectly fine," she replied breathlessly, laying a hand to her chest, her heart thumping like a tinner's hammer.

Oh, how she wished she could go back in time so that she could be standing before the window, awash in the morning sun, looking dewy and serene rather than disheveled and rampant with lustful thoughts.

As usual, Derek was perfectly tailored, ever the English peer and Highland laird, a man who commanded others and undoubtedly never knew a single fear. Which was not surprising, with that tall, ruggedly built frame. If the man possessed an ounce of fat, Rosalyn defied anyone to find it.

"My lady?"

Rosalyn's head jerked up from drinking him in, and she felt that dratted heat blossom in her cheeks. He must think her an utter loon.

Had she known that Derek was actually thinking she was the most stunning creature he had encountered in his thirty-one years, her concerns might have been allayed.

He had never seen hair as she had, like spun gold, wild now from her tumble from the trunk and haloed around her head, the sun backlighting her, bringing to mind a stained-glass image that had captivated him as a child.

The window rested over the altar in their chapel at Glen Cairn, which sat high atop a crag on Castle Gray's property.

The glass had come all the way from a master craftsman in Belgium and had been fussed over as though it was the Holy Grail. Derek had watched as the heavy glass piece, with its kaleidoscope of colors, was lifted high into the air and shifted gently into its spot, fitting in place as though it had always belonged there.

Long after his father and the workmen had left, Derek had stood staring up at the woman forever etched in the panes.

Her head was turned slightly over one porcelain shoulder, her blond hair flowing down her back like a river of gold. The sun in the upper corner of the frame shone down on her, her billowing white dress glimmering as her soft wings spread to catch the sun's warmth.

Her profile was as flawless as a Greek coin, yet a hint of a mischievous grin teased her lips. She was an angel with an impish side, sent down from heaven to bring light into the dark.

Derek had always found comfort with her when his parents were arguing, as they often did while he was growing up, and she had given him strength during the conflicts between the clans—conflicts that never seemed to end. That was the very reason for his hasty trip to London: to settle his mother's property and put England behind him.

His loyalty to Scotland had been questioned from the moment of his birth since his mother was an English lady. Now that he governed the clan, he had to show them once and for all where his loyalty lay.

"My lord?" Rosalyn queried tentatively, wondering what thoughts were running through

Derek's mind as his gaze was fastened so fiercely on her. To be the sole focus of all that unwavering attention was disconcerting.

He stared at her for another heartbeat and then shifted abruptly on the balls of his feet and closed her bedroom door, isolating them from the world.

Rosalyn's mouth went dry, and her heart beat like a hummingbird's wings. She was completely alone with him—six-plus feet of glorious virility that even a saint could not overlook.

Rosalyn lifted her chin. "I presume you wish to speak privately to me, my lord?"

"Derek." He leaned a shoulder against her bed-post. "There are to be no formalities between us."

He had said that before—right after she had shamelessly kissed him in the Senhavens' garden, behind an overgrown rosebush whose lush fragrance Rosalyn found herself recalling every night in her dreams—along with the taste and texture of his mouth, which her gaze kept drifting to.

"We need to discuss last night's visitor."

"What is there to discuss? As you can see, I'm perfectly fine." No good would come of worrying another person. She had made her decision and would stick by it.

His gaze ran slowly over her, bringing an unexpected heat to those places. "I'm not so sure about that. Perhaps I should check?"

Rosalyn's heart missed a beat as she searched for her voice. "While I appreciate your diligence, I—"

"Going somewhere?" he interjected, his gaze shifting to her trunk, where a pair of lacy pantalets trailed from the open top. Rosalyn hastily tucked them in and prayed her mortification didn't show on her face.

Meeting his gaze, she replied, "I intend to take a trip."

He quirked a single dark eyebrow. "Really? And where had you planned to go?"

Rosalyn frowned at him, not appreciating the amused light in his eyes that said he knew she had nowhere to go.

"I don't know precisely, but you needn't worry. I have several ideas."

"Such as?" he prompted, moving close enough that she could see how perfectly shaven he was, though a shadow would surely darken his chin by sunset.

There was something enigmatic about him, a quality she could not quite describe. Dangerous, perhaps? Yet that seemed inadequate. Maybe it was his restless air. He reminded her of a caged tiger, and when she was around him, she felt like a tigress.

She started as a hand gently cupped her chin. There was an oddly tender expression on his face. "No one is going to hurt you," he murmured. "I won't allow it." He held her like that for a moment, then dropped his hand away, his brows drawing together, and his voice turning brusque. "Get whatever you need together, then meet me downstairs."

He headed for the door, but Rosalyn's question stopped him on the threshold. "Where are we going?"

He glanced at her over his shoulder. "To Scotland."

"Scotland? You must be mistaken. I cannot go to Scotland."

"As I see it, you have no other choice." He walked out the door.

Rosalyn headed after him, but Clarisse suddenly appeared and took her by the arm. "Don't fight him, my dear. He will get what he wants. He always does."

Rosalyn stood in a state of confusion. "I can't go to Scotland. What can he be thinking?"

"Of your safety."

"I barely know him!"

"Not from what I've seen. There's enough heat between the two of you to set this house ablaze. Since your arrival in London, you have spent more time with Derek than any of the other men who have been desperately trying to get your attention—which, in case you haven't noticed, has been greatly diminished with Derek continually at your side. The word is that you have been claimed, my dear."

Rosalyn took a deep breath. That was what she had feared. She was disturbingly attracted to him, but she could not allow that to cloud her judgment or imperil him.

"I can't go. Don't you see? I won't involve another person in my problem."

Clarisse laid a hand on her shoulder and turned Rosalyn around. "If there is one individual that I would feel secure entrusting with your care, it's Derek. He won't allow anything to happen to you. He will find your stepbrother and end his machinations. You could look upon this trip as a new experience. The Highlands are really quite lovely this time of year."

The feeling of being trapped pressed in on Rosalyn. "His lordship is an unmarried man, and I am an unmarried female. That precludes us from traveling together."

"Do you believe Derek would extend such an invitation were he not prepared to provide you with an appropriate chaperone?"

"An invitation?" Rosalyn harrumphed. "It sounded more like a demand to my ears."

"Derek has never been a man who takes no for an answer," Clarisse conceded with a shrug.

A sense of desperation rose up in Rosalyn as she paced to the opposite side of the room and swung around. "Surely there must be some other solution? Something we're overlooking?" Yet she knew she had exhausted every avenue during the long night without sleep.

It was either go to Scotland with his lordship and pray he could convince Calder to leave her be, or move from place to place, hoping to outdistance her stepbrother—a prospect she did not relish.

Clarisse took her hand, sympathy on her face. "Trust me," she said softly. "You need more protection than I can provide, as proven by last night's debacle. Derek's home is like a fortress. His men number in the hundreds. Not even a mouse could squeak by without his notice. Please, my dear, say you'll go. Neither my heart nor my peace of mind will be appeased until I know you are safe."

Rosalyn chewed a corner of her lip, riddled with conflict. She did not wish further worry upon Clarisse. But what of Derek? Did he realize what he was getting himself into? Calder would not stop until his plan had been brought to fruition.

Rosalyn closed her eyes, worn to the marrow with the turmoil her stepbrother was wreaking on her life. She seemed to move in ever smaller circles to stay out of his reach, and she could not go on like this.

She had to go, she realized with a sinking heart. What other choice did she have? Calder had found her, and neither Lady Dane nor anyone in her household would be safe until Rosalyn was gone.

Rosalyn sighed. "You're right, of course. His lordship has offered me sanctuary; it would be foolish not to accept his kindness." Temporarily.

"I'll finish packing my things. Please tell Lord Manchester I will be down shortly."

Clarisse smiled warmly at her. "You're making the right decision, my dear. Derek will take good care of you. He won't let any harm befall you."

Rosalyn watched Clarisse leave, her step buoyant now that she believed the problem solved. But Rosalyn knew differently. And as she turned to finish packing her belongings, she wondered, who would protect Derek while he was protecting her?

Three

"Ye've lost your mind, lad. What could y' be thinkin' tae allow this woman tae come tae Castle Gray—and not just any woman, mind y', but an *Englishwoman*? 'Twill be the end of all of us. Mark my words."

Derek ignored his uncle's characteristic prophecies of doom. Darius, his father's only surviving brother, tended to forget that Derek was no longer a child and therefore no longer in need of his guidance.

Granted, this time his uncle was probably right. Bringing Rosalyn back to his home would undoubtedly cause a stir, and with the current unrest, the last thing he needed was another complication.

He wasn't worried about her stepbrother. In fact, he hoped the sod found out where she was. Should Calder—now Lord Westcott—set foot on Derek's property, the man would promptly find himself footless.

Derek raised his hand to forestall his uncle from going off on another tear. "Enough, Darius. The girl is coming with us, and that's the end of the matter."

"Why are y' bein' so hardheaded? Since when are y' the type tae be savin' damsels in distress I'd like tae know? Should the Trelawnys get wind of it, they may think you've gone soft."

"And is that what you think, Uncle? That I've gone soft?"

"Of course not, lad," Darius blustered. "Ye're hard as nails. But I cannae help wondering what good will come of havin' this English lass in our midst. Y' remember how hard it was for your mother, God rest her soul."

If any laird had been unyielding and uncompromising, it had been Derek's father. His mother had been the epitome of a gently bred English miss. Two people could not have been from more contradictory backgrounds.

Derek had often wondered what his mother had seen in William McDougal. His father had more closely resembled a barbarian, with his wild, knotted hair that reached to the middle of his back.

If that had not been enough to scare off the meek at heart, then the distant promontories that jutted up around Castle Gray, like swords thrusting straight out of hell, would. Most people who visited promptly acquired a sudden need to flee in the other direction.

His home on the northernmost point of the Highlands was a place no outsider, least of all a woman, wanted to come. The harsh terrain had been no place for his mother, though for a while, she had tried to make it work.

His parents had loved each other once, but love could not stem the loss that came when they realized they both had mountains the other couldn't climb.

That was when the arguments began, and the endless recriminations and bitterness. When Derek's father began grooming him to take his place as laird, his mother had returned to England, leaving Derek to be shuttled back and forth between two homes—and constantly forced to choose between his parents and his countries.

To please his mother he had taken his lofty English title and surname, but his life belonged in Scotland. He loved its fierce beauty: the uncompromising landscape, the pristine skies, the harsh weather that could rattle a man down to the bone.

What would Rosalyn see? Would she find his country barren and distasteful? Or might she view it as he did?

His questions vanished as the front door of Lady Dane's town house opened and a vision in a rose-hued day dress stepped out onto the landing, her chin high as though she were being led to the guillotine. She was terrified but would not show it. God, she was fascinating.

Derek ground his cheroot beneath his boot heel and pushed away from the coach, tamping down the nagging sensation in the pit of his belly that asked him what the hell he was doing. Darius was right. It wasn't in his nature to concern himself with other people's troubles; he had enough of his own.

He could have secured other means for her protection. He had not needed to get directly involved. There were plenty of people who owed him favors, but he had not even considered their help.

He could already be on his way back home rather than walking up the steps to take hold of Rosalyn's hand, which trembled slightly beneath his fingertips. Yet with that simple touch and the look of trust in her beautiful blue eyes, Derek knew he had to do this for her. There was no fighting it.

"Are you ready?" he asked gently.

Rosalyn hesitated, uncertainty sluicing through her before her concerns were calmed by the look in Derek's eyes. There was something about his relaxed posture and slight smile that told her that she had nothing to fear—except her unusual attraction for him. If she wasn't careful, she would find herself doing something very foolhardy, like kissing him again.

Taking a breath, she replied, "I am, my lord. And thank you for your assistance in this . . . bothersome situation."

"Shall we go?"

"Yes, of course." Rosalyn turned to Clarisse. "Thank you for all you've done."

"May your journey find you happier at its end, my dear. You know I will be here to help with whatever you need, whenever you need it."

Rosalyn took hold of her hand. "I don't know what I would have done without you. Had I never taken that first step out of Cornwall, I wouldn't have met you."

"Nor I, you. And that would have been a terrible shame." Patting Rosalyn's hand, she said gently, "Now go on with you. I'm sure his lordship is eager to get some ground under him before night falls."

"If you see Fancy—"

"Ease your mind, my dear. I will make sure she knows you're safe." She leaned over to whisper, "Trust Derek. He will see you through this."

Rosalyn tried to smile. "I will."

Clarisse straightened. "Good. Now off with you." With a sheen of tears in her eyes, her hostess shooed her into the coach.

Rosalyn continued to look back until Clarisse was no more than a speck in the distance. Her throat closed and she felt on the verge of tears, but crying would solve nothing, and Derek would undoubtedly think her a supreme nuisance.

"You'll see her again."

Derek sat across from her, looking incredibly large with his tall, broad form taking up most of the seat, and his long legs brushing her skirts each time the coach hit a bump.

"I know," Rosalyn replied, hating the waver in her voice. "Will the trip take very long?"

"About two days."

She hadn't expected such a long journey. She recalled that she had been promised an appropriate chaperone, who did not appear to be with them.

As though reading her thoughts, Derek remarked, "Once we reached Castle Gray, your needs will be seen to by one of the maids."

She would be without another female for two days—two days of overwhelming temptation. Her stomach fluttered and her palms grew clammy whenever Derek was near her—and for two days, he would be very near. Sweet heavens.

"It's to be just the two of us?"

"No, my uncle is with us. He hates all forms of transportation other than his own horse, no matter how grueling the journey."

Rosalyn wished she had the freedom to ride herself; it had always soothed her.

She started as Derek took hold of her right hand. "What have you done here?" Gently, he brushed a finger across a tender spot on her palm.

"It's nothing." She tried to disengage her hand, but he would not let go. "It's really very silly. I was practicing my parries and thrusts in my room last night."

"You fence?"

Rosalyn had hoped he would accept her answer and move on. "Not exactly. Rather I was practicing with a fire poker."

"I see," he said, trying not to smile. "And do you do this poker fencing often?"

Rosalyn glared at him. "No, I do not. But I must have some method of defense against my stepbrother."

He lost the battle to keep his grin at bay, which made her want to toss something at him. The man could be utterly maddening.

Her annoyance was diverted as his thumb began to stroke back and forth across the top of her hand, making her skin tingle before his fingers slowly slipped from hers.

Rosalyn could still feel his caress as she settled back against the velvet squabs and forced her attention to the scenery passing her window.

As the coach traveled farther from London, the overcrowded streets and jumble of buildings began to fade into the wild beauty of the countryside, creating a feeling of wistful longing inside her.

She missed Meadows Cove, where she and Fancy had spent so many lazy afternoons watching fishing boats bob on the windswept tide, sitting in the shadows of the old gnarled oak with their toes dug into the cool sand, watching the sandpipers dashing among the willowy reeds while concocting grand stories about buried treasures in the caves that dotted the cliffs.

These made-up tales came replete with handsome buccaneers riding the waves to shore, or dastardly pirates seeking shelter from the regulation men who sought to end their illegal trade.

It was images of pirates that occupied Rosalyn's mind as her eyelids slowly drifted shut—pirates with eyes bluer than a Caribbean sea, and hair dark as midnight.

Scottish pirates wearing kilts and little else.

Derek watched Rosalyn fight the pull of her own exhaustion until she finally fell into a deep sleep.

He couldn't remember the last time a woman

had so fully captured his attention. Or aroused him. But he was Rosalyn's protector now, and he couldn't take advantage of her under the guise of helping her.

Even the most licentious of his fellow Pleasure Seekers, Hunter Manning, would not do such a thing. There were many reasons why Hunter was called "Notorious"; his ability to slip in and out of any woman's boudoir without notice was the least of them.

Derek doubted there was a woman alive who would ever snare the rogue. He was well versed in the tricks that could land a fellow in a state of matrimony, yet that never stopped females from throwing themselves at him.

Derek would be damned if he could figure out his friend's appeal. The man was cynical and didn't trust women as a general rule; he considered them wolves in fashionable clothing. Derek doubted there was a woman in existence who could rock his friend back on his heels, but he hoped he was around if it ever happened.

Nevertheless, none of them would take advantage of a vulnerable female. And despite Rosalyn's brave face, she was a scared girl in an untenable position. Derek was impressed with how well she had held up. Another woman might have barricaded herself in her room in a constant swoon, jumping at every noise. Not Rosalyn.

Derek smiled as he remembered the sight that greeted him when he barged into Rosalyn's bedroom, half expecting to find her engaged in a scuffle with another kidnapper.

Waist-length blond hair swung like a pendulum against her slender back as she bounced up and down on the lid of a trunk, bits of clothing and frilly undergarments spilling over the edge.

But what had left Derek momentarily speechless was the vision she made when she stood up, her beautiful face flushed from exertion and her body garbed in a demure but shape-revealing day dress.

The sight had nearly stopped his heart. He had wanted to gather her in his arms and do all the things that had been tormenting his mind since laying eyes on her—touch her all over, make her hum with desire. But she was a lady, sweet, guileless, and unschooled in the ways of men. Yet how he longed to teach her . . .

Perhaps what was even more amazing about

her was that she had no idea how glorious she looked. If he asked her if she thought herself beautiful, she would scoff—but no man who laid eyes on her would miss it.

Yet during the few weeks that Derek had known her, he had found himself looking beyond the beauty on the outside and enjoying what was on the inside more: the simple pleasure of her company, the musical cadence of her laugh, her gentle wit. He had been entranced—and continued to be.

The coach began to slow, and Derek glanced out the window, realizing how much time had passed. The sun had begun to set in a fiery red ball sinking below the horizon as they came to a stop in front of the George and Dragon, a quaint inn with an ample supply of ale and an even more ample supply of barmaids. He had made this stop frequently over the years, and while the idea of a warm female in his bed was a tempting one, he dismissed it.

"We've arrived, m'lord," his driver bellowed as he swung open the coach door.

"Quiet, man," Derek growled, nodding toward Rosalyn's sleeping form. He knew she hadn't gotten much rest the night before; he had heard her pacing her room. Nearly a half dozen times he had caught himself heading toward the door, wanting nothing more than to take her in his arms and tell her everything would be all right.

"Sorry, y'r lordship," the driver said in a whisper. "Would y' like me tae get a man tae carry the lady tae her room?"

"What am I?" Derek muttered stiffly, sweeping past his driver with Rosalyn held snugly against his chest.

He frowned at how insubstantial she felt. He had not missed the fact that she had grown thinner; he needed to get a few of his cook's good meals in her.

He entered the tavern and was promptly greeted by the proprietor, who smiled broadly as he waddled over to him. "Ah, your lordship. So glad to have you back. Will you be staying long?"

"Just the night."

Disappointment was evident on the proprietor's face. "And who is the lovely young miss?"

Though Derek should have been prepared for the question, surprisingly, he wasn't. "She's a relative in need of a quiet place to rest."

The innkeeper scratched his jaw and squinted an eye at Rosalyn. "A relative, you say?" The fact that she looked nothing like Derek was not lost on the portly man, but he wisely kept his thoughts to himself. "I've got a perfect spot for your, er . . . ?"

"Cousin," Derek supplied without missing a beat.

"Aye. Your cousin. Will you be needing separate rooms, then?"

"Yes, two rooms."

The innkeeper nodded and trundled up the stairs. At the end of the hallway, he threw open a door. "There y' go." He waved Derek inside. "The best room in the house."

"Best" seemed a loose term as Derek glanced around the small space, furnished with only the barest necessities. He wanted Rosalyn to be comfortable.

"I'd like a tub and hot water brought up. My cousin might wish for a bath should she awaken."

"I'll get right on it, your lordship. Your room is right through there." He gestured to an adjoining door, and Derek wasn't sure whether to thank the man for making his life easier or throttle him for putting temptation within his grasp. "Might there be anything else you require?"

"Food," Derek answered. "And lots of it."

The man bobbed his head obediently and backed out of the room.

Laying Rosalyn on the bed, Derek stepped back to look at her. She shifted to her side, her slender hands sliding up to prop beneath her cheek, a thin beam of light washing her face in a golden glow, highlighting her pale beauty and making her appear almost ethereal.

His thoughts were not nearly so heavenly. He imagined slowly stripping the clothes from her body, bringing her awake with his mouth on hers, looking into her dewy blue eyes as his hands cupped her beautiful breasts, so round and ripe, a bounty on such a petite frame.

Her gaze would stay upon him as she took her hand and guided his shaft into her tight passage, moaning low as he slipped voluptuously into her, pausing tenderly at her maidenhead before breaking through and claiming her, his body wracked in an agony of enjoyment.

He would rock in and out of her, plunge to the hilt and ease all the way out, over and over again, holding himself in check as he felt the signs of her ardor, her warm, wet vault closing tighter around him, squeezing, drawing him in, her nails digging into his back as she urged him on until she reached orgasm, her cry of pleasure ringing in his ears.

Derek sucked in a deep breath, his trousers molding an erection that bordered on painful as he opened a window to cool his heated body. Daily his thoughts grew more indecent, his body more randy. Rosalyn was a lady and must be treated as such. He did not want to scare her.

He glanced down at her sleeping form and thought she looked like an angel. Derek wondered if she always slept so deeply or if sheer exhaustion had taken hold of her. He resisted a childish need to wake her, if for no other reason than to talk to her. She never failed to entertain him with her stories.

A knock at the door brought him around in time to see his uncle pop his head in. "The lass is asleep, I see."

"Your powers of observation are remarkable," Derek drawled as he undid his cufflinks and pocketed them.

"Don't get snide now, lad. I was only makin' sure she was well."

"Next time, wait for your knock to be answered. She could have been undressing."

The corner of Darius's lip lifted in a grin. "And I suspect that would have been a fetchin' sight indeed." Derek's scowl did not deter his uncle. "While we're on the topic, why are *you* in here? Does your fair 'cousin' require a maid to brush her flaxen hair? 'Tis quite the image; the mighty laird playin' lady's maid."

"You stretch the boundaries of my patience, uncle."

Darius scoffed. "All bark, y' are, lad. If the Trelawny boys knew what a soft touch y' were, I suspect ye'd have found yourself dethroned by now."

The only person who had ever found Derek remotely soft was his uncle, and that was only because Derek had treated him with the deference due him for his age.

"They're welcome to try," Derek replied. "Since you're feeling so sage, perhaps you can shed some light on who's behind the odd things that have been going on lately."

Darius straightened, his bushy brows yanked together in a deep frown. "Are ye implyin' I'm a traitor?"

Derek had no patience left for his uncle's endless dramatics, and snapped, "The question is a straightforward one. You have as much to gain from seeing me dead as anyone."

His uncle's hand tightened around the doorknob. "I'll pretend I didn't hear the question, then. And may your beloved father, God rest him, never know what ye have asked me this day. Good night tae ye."

Four

Derek ran a hand through his hair and cursed softly. What a bloody damn day. First kidnappers, now this. He didn't want to contemplate what might happen next.

He wasn't sure what had motivated him to accuse Darius of being disloyal. His uncle had always been there for him. He had mentored Derek when his own father had been too busy, and he had seen him through some of the toughest times of his life. When Derek had finally accepted his rightful duty and taken his father's place as laird, Darius had crowed like a rooster. He would have to apologize in the morning. Now, however, he had to see to his charge.

Derek turned back to the bed, expecting to find Rosalyn still asleep, but discovered drowsy blue eyes fixed on him in curiosity.

"Where are we?" she murmured, her hair tumbled around her head like a golden cloud, making Derek itch to run his fingers through it. He had not been able to resist twining a length around his hand when he carried her upstairs.

"We're at an inn on the outskirts of the northern border."

She sat up against the pillows. "Did you stop because of me?"

"Not at all." Though in truth, she had been his main concern. He was used to covering a lot of ground before stopping, but the trip would have taken too much of a toll on her.

She appeared so fragile, and he wondered how well she would hold up. Perhaps he should have taken her somewhere else, or left her with someone else. He hadn't been thinking clearly. There was more than just the reaction of his clan to consider. There was Megan, too.

He had known Megan since they were children, and though they were from opposing clans, the strife had not affected them. Oh, he'd tried to act tough with her. An eight-year-old boy pretending to be a mighty warlord, and she all of five years old and following him around, thinking he was ridiculous but worth the effort nonetheless. As the years rolled by, he had come to value her friendship.

What would she think of his new houseguest?

"We normally stop here before going on," he said. "The terrain along the coastline can be dangerous after dark, and there are the border clans to consider."

Her brows drew lightly together. "Border clans?"

Derek glanced out the window into the cloudless night, the moon cresting over the shadowed branches of the trees.

"There are four border clans, and they fiercely monitor who is coming and going, especially if they get a whiff they're English."

"Why does it make a difference if the person is English? The discord between England and Scotland no longer exists."

"It exists in the mind of some persistent Scots. We have long memories and tend to cling to our ways. Scots can be a suspicious lot by nature."

"You say 'we.' Do you consider yourself Scottish,

then? You seem far more English. Your speech is impeccable."

Derek turned toward her and leaned his shoulder against the wall, something about her words rubbing a raw spot in him. "Despite this gentlemanly exterior, I *am* one of those heathenish Scots."

Some of the enjoyment dimmed from her eyes, and Derek cursed himself, knowing she had not been passing judgment as so many others, but merely speaking out of curiosity.

"I speak as I do because it makes things easier," he said, "and I prefer to be troubled as little as possible."

"I understand." She looked away from him to fiddle with the sleeve of her dress.

"And what is it you think you understand?"

She slanted a quick sideways glance at him. "That you believe I will be trouble. You needn't worry, I'm fully capable of taking care of myself. So should you wish to travel on without me, I will be just fine."

Derek caught himself before he smiled. The lass was not only brave but stubborn, and perhaps had a healthy dose of temper, which might prove interesting.

"Do you always jump to conclusions?" he asked, shouldering away from the wall and stopping at the edge of the bed, watching her eyes widen with each step he took.

He trailed a finger along her cheek, leaving Rosalyn unable to catch hold of a single thought as he loomed over her, large and rugged.

In the dim light, with whiskers dusting his jaw and his hair slightly wild, she could tell that his claim was not an idle one. He was not the refined gentleman she had believed. He had merely done as society expected of him while he was among it.

Now that he was away from London, he could be himself—the very prospect made Rosalyn shiver. She had believed he would be the courteous and polite man he had been thus far, if not somewhat removed. Looking in his eyes now, she saw a banked heat, and everything inside her responded to it.

She wet her lips. "If I'm mistaken, please forgive me. I simply don't wish to be a burden."

"Have I made you feel as though you were?" he asked, his voice slipping over her like silk.

"No, but—"

"Will you trust me?" His gaze met hers, and

all her concerns were allayed. She might not completely understand him, but she did trust him.

Rosalyn nodded.

"Good," he murmured, cupping her cheek, his thumb smoothing across her skin, making her want to close her eyes and lean into the warmth of his palm.

The moment was broken by a knock on the door. Derek lowered his hand before turning toward the door and saying gruffly, "Come."

A portly man poked his head in. "Her ladyship's bath is ready, my lord. May we bring it in?"

Derek waved the man inside.

The proprietor was followed by two boys, their cherubic faces smudged with dirt and their small feet bare. Rosalyn's heart went out to them. They should be in bed by now, not carting water for her bath. It would feel divine, no doubt, but was unnecessary, as she had bathed just that morning.

Tossing her legs over the side of the bed, she moved to her pelisse jacket and retrieved her beaded purse. Pulling out two coins, she turned to give each boy the money, but was stopped by a hand to her wrist. She glanced up to find Derek scowling at her.

"Put it away, madam," he told her in a voice that brooked no argument.

"But I—"

"I will attend to the matter." He spoke calmly, but the steely look in his eyes said something far different.

He turned from her and ushered the boys and the proprietor out the door. He stood with them for a moment, a low-voiced conversation ensuing before the door slowly clicked shut.

Leaving her alone with him.

Again.

Need blazed anew, images of him bathing her—or bathing with her, stroking a warm, wet cloth over her shoulders and chest—and lower.

But one glance told her that bathing—with or without her—was the last thing on his mind. Tension radiated from his tall frame as he regarded her through hooded eyes. "You will never go into your own purse again for anything. Do you understand? If you require something, you will come to me."

Rosalyn stared at him, taken aback by his vehemence and his audacity. She was not without means or the ability to decide how those funds would be disbursed. The coins would not pauper her and it surely would have helped those two boys.

"I could not have heard you correctly."

"You heard me correctly."

"I will not be told what to do."

"So noted. Now, do you need any help undressing?"

His lightning-quick switch of topic left Rosalyn momentarily unbalanced. "Excuse me?"

"There must be at least two dozen buttons to undo. Why they make women's clothing so confounding, I'll never know. Little pearl beards running from your neck to your—" He frowned. "Makes no bloody sense."

The prospect of him helping her undress was both appealing and unnerving. "I don't know what you could be thinking, my lord. If you're expecting some kind of repayment for your generosity, I will thank you, but no more."

He stared at her for a moment, then tipped his head back and laughed. "You think I'm trying to seduce you?" He gestured to the tub. "I merely intended to assist you while the water is still hot."

The man was positively wretched. Couldn't he have just said what he intended from the start?

"Thank you for the offer, but if you'll be so kind to send a maid, I'm sure I'll be fine."

He shook his head. "No maids here, I'm afraid."

"There must be one. Any woman will do—the proprietor's wife, perhaps?"

"He doesn't have one."

"A barmaid, then? You aren't going to tell me there aren't any of them?"

"There are plenty, but none that you'll want helping you."

"And why is that?"

"They have a penchant for robbing people blind."

Rosalyn scoffed. "The innkeeper would never let such a thing happen."

Derek cocked an eyebrow. "The proprietor splits whatever they take."

Rosalyn stared at him. "You mean he condones what they do?"

"He insists upon it. Did the man look like a saint to you?"

Rosalyn had never been one to pass judgment with a glance, but it was true that the innkeeper did have a particularly beady way about him, and there was something moderately sinister about his thin lips, and the way he had peered at her when he left had been a bit chilling. It had reminded her of the way Calder had always looked at her.

Rosalyn lifted her chin. "If what you're saying is true, then why do you stay here?"

"Because the man knows better than to consider me a pigeon for his plucking."

Though his tone was calm, Rosalyn shivered. How had she not seen it before? He *was* dangerous. He should come with a sign that warned away the unwary.

"Well," she said, hands on hips, "I guess I'll have to do for myself."

Derek crossed his arms over his chest with a devilish half-grin. "Are you sure?"

Her heart missed a beat. "Positive."

He sighed. "I've been dismissed, then." The way he trudged toward the door was so comical, Rosalyn had to suppress her laugh. He glanced over his shoulder as he gripped the doorknob. "If there's nothing else I can do?"

Rosalyn felt oddly discontent to see him leave. "Well, there is one thing."

The way his eyebrows rose told her what he thought that one thing was. She frowned at him, and he had the good sense to look chagrined. "And what is that?"

Rosalyn nibbled her lower lip. "This may sound strange, but . . ."

"Yes?"

"Well, I've always been curious about the lives of working women."

He looked confused. "Why?"

"I'd like to know what it's like to make my own money."

"Don't wish for something you would not want. The days are long, and the work is thankless. Any of them would give their eyeteeth to trade places with you."

"I've thought about writing on the subject—you know, from a female's perspective. Have you ever noticed that all the newspaper articles are from a man's point of view?"

Derek chuckled. "It's not exactly a new concept, I'm afraid."

"So surely it's time for a change."

"And you think you can effect this change?"

"Do you think I can't?"

"I have no doubt you can do anything you put your mind to, but historically, women writers have been verbally stoned. Such a female would have to be very tough to survive the slings and arrows."

"I'm much tougher than I look." Rosalyn lifted her chin.

Those cobalt blue eyes gave her a thoroughly wicked appraisal.

Heat and indignation rose inside her. "I wasn't referring to physical toughness, my lord."

"But you must admit that you don't exactly look the rugged type."

"And what type do I look like?"

"The truth?"

"Of course."

"You look . . . pampered. I can't imagine you've had a day of hard labor in your life."

Rosalyn stared at him, shocked and hurt by his assessment. "Pampered? I'll have you know that I have never been pampered in my entire life. I spent a good portion of my life on the Cornish coast—not the type of place for cosseted females."

"There's no need to defend yourself to me. You were born a lady. I wouldn't expect you to know any other life than what you've lived."

He didn't seem to believe a lady had a great deal of worth. Well, she would show him quite differently.

"I'm far more capable than you imagine."

"And I look forward to your revealing each and every one of those capabilities." His remark sounded seductive, matching the gleam in his eyes. "But I believe you were extolling the virtues of the working female?"

"I was merely saying that I'd like to know more about these women's daily lives. Perhaps if someone exposed the conditions under which they were forced to work, it could bring about a change."

"It's a nice thought, but it won't happen."

"And why not?"

"Because people would have to give a damn, and few do."

"I do. In fact, I could start my research with the women here."

"These particular females are not the type you would associate with."

"And why is that? Stealing is nothing I fear."

"It is not the stealing that concerns me. Rather that they cater to the male patrons."

"Cater?"

"Service is perhaps more appropriate."

The image of a woman on her knees and a man with a carnal look on his face washed through Rosalyn's mind. "Oh." A blush heated her cheeks.

Derek laughed. "Oh, indeed."

Rosalyn put her hands on her hips, not amused. "And I imagine you know these women's talents firsthand?"

She wasn't sure what prompted her to ask the question, or why the idea of Derek in the arms of one of the tavern's barmaids even bothered her. He didn't belong to her, just as she didn't belong to him. But how she wanted to.

He leaned down, shockingly close to her face, his warm breath fanning her neck, his lips only a hair's breadth from her ear, as he said in a deceptively soft voice, "The answer is no. I have never dallied with any of the barmaids. Does that ease your mind?"

"My mind is perfectly at ease." It was her body that felt oddly tense. "But we were speaking about the barmaids' plight. I doubt they really want to steal or . . ." Warmth flooded her cheeks. "Do that other thing."

"Sex is a very natural thing between a man and woman, you know."

She prayed her thoughts didn't show on her face. "Of course. Nevertheless, that doesn't mean I could make love to a man without loving him."

The silence that followed her comment fell in thick waves around her, and Rosalyn suspected Derek found her provincial and ridiculous.

She was not so innocent that she didn't understand that people coupled purely for pleasure. She suspected Derek did it all the time. He didn't appear to be a man who denied his physical needs.

"Your commitment is admirable," he finally

said. "You should hold on to your beliefs. Do not give away what you have to offer; the right man would do anything to have you."

The intensity in his eyes took her breath away. "You really think so?" she asked softly.

"Yes." Then he leaned down and kissed her.

Rosalyn felt on fire, flames of need licking at her skin, clamoring to be appeased. The things a simple kiss could do, the exquisite pressure he created as his lips slanted over hers, wrung soft moans from deep in her throat. She felt on edge, like a foreigner in her own body.

She tenuously slid her hands over his shoulders, following the sleek, muscled contours to his neck to entwine her fingers in his thick, silky hair as she had wanted to do for weeks.

The ache that had begun in her chest became a dull throb between her thighs, building with every sweep of his tongue.

He broke the contact, taking a step back, then another, as though trying to escape. Rosalyn was grateful. He was too masculine and beautiful, too much of a temptation. And even though he might feel desire for her, nothing could ever come of it.

"It's late," he said in a raspy voice.

"Yes," she whispered, wrapping her arms around her waist.

Without another word, he strode to the door. It opened and shut with the barest sound. He was gone, only the faint smell of sandalwood left to mark his place.

Five

Derek paced the scarred floorboards of the darkened tavern the next morning. Several patrons snored away their overindulgence, while the clock that hung askew upon the wall kept time with the rhythmic click of his boot heels. His gaze continued to move to the stairs leading to the rooms above, from where Rosalyn had yet to emerge.

He'd had a restless night, roaming the confines of his room, listening for any sound coming from Rosalyn's side of the door. Her safety had not been the only thing on his mind—the sweetness of her kiss had haunted him.

His growing desire for her had kept him in a sexual stranglehold, and he had finally forced himself to his bed until the sun crept over the horizon.

He had been so damn sure he could mentally beat his attraction to her into submission. He never realized how difficult it would be.

"A drink to calm your nerves, my lord?"

The innkeeper held up a tray with a large mug of ale on it. Derek took the mug and tossed a handful of coins on the tray.

With a greedy smile, the proprietor counted his earnings as he trundled off to the kitchen to bark orders at his help.

Derek took a sip of the foul-tasting brew and grimaced. Sheep's piss. What had he expected? No one could make ale like Highlanders, and his clan made the best beer in all of Scotland.

Rich, dark hops were aged in thick oak barrels until properly ripe. People traveled great distances just for a taste. Their ale was part of a plan he had implemented to restock the clan's coffers, which his father had greatly depleted waging battles against rival clans.

His father had been a good leader, but too

much hot blood ran in his veins. He had been fond of telling Derek that he would never be a truly great laird because of his English stock.

Derek had resisted the urge to remind his father that the choice of his origin had not been his own. His father enjoyed a selective memory, preferring to believe that Derek had been conceived by means other than the usual—and when drunk, he would go a step further and accuse his wife of being unfaithful.

Derek remembered how much time he had spent hating himself as a child and wondering how two people who disliked each other so much had ever become man and wife.

He forced back the memory and turned toward the stairs as footfalls descended. A figure emerged from the shadows, but not the person he had been waiting for.

The woman's back was slightly humped and her face even more aged than her years. He had hired her from a nearby village that morning, offering her a good deal of money to assist Rosalyn.

"The lass be right down, m'lord," she said with a wheeze. "And may I say the gel is quite luvely. If only me own daughters could be so fair, perhaps I could find them proper suitors." She sighed, resigned to her fate. "If that is all y' be needin' . . . ?"

"Yes," Derek replied distractedly, his gaze drifting to the staircase.

"Then good day tae y', sir. Remember old Martha when next y're in town."

Derek barely heard a word she said as delicate steps made a slow progression down the stairs. Every muscle in his body tensed, and an uncharacteristic agitation stole over him. Since meeting Rosalyn, he couldn't seem to shake the effect she had on him.

"Well, well. If it ain't King Manchester," a voice drawled behind him.

Derek's hands fisted at his sides as he pivoted to face the person speaking to him—a man he could barely tolerate most days, and whom he had often contemplated severing completely from his life. The task might have proved easier had the man not been his brother—or half-brother, actually. His father had strayed often, if the tales were true, but none of the women had offered up a babe, except one.

"What are you doing here?" Derek asked tightly, endeavoring to keep his anger in check. His brother had an uncanny way of showing up at the most inopportune times. Ethan's sole purpose in life seemed to be annoying him, and he succeeded far better than Derek would ever let on.

"What kind of greeting is that for your beloved sibling? Surely you're happy to see me?"

Derek refused to get reeled in. Ethan enjoyed prodding him until they were a hair's breadth from exchanging blows, always making it look as though Derek had lost his temper first, or that Derek begrudged his brother what Ethan deemed his rightful heritage.

Some of his clan were actually sympathetic to Ethan. He was a bastard, never recognized by his father, and ironically the one person who had real reason to shun him was the very person who made sure he was educated and left a small inheritance: Derek's mother.

Lady Emmaline had refused to be pitied or looked at as a laughingstock because her husband had flaunted his transgressions. Instead she had used those very transgressions, tossing them up in his face at every opportunity. And what better way to do that than to raise the son he refused to acknowledge?

To further the irony, Ethan was really more deserving of being the laird than Derek. Ethan was firstborn, bastard or not. And Ethan's mother had been a Scottish princess, though her clan had lost most of their prosperity in her early days.

In the fifteen years after Ethan's birth, his mother's clan had become a nomadic group, primarily scavengers and peddlers and vagabonds. Most Scottish found their presence a blight, and they were often treated like the lowest forms of humanity.

When Ethan had first come to live with them, Derek had felt sorry for his half-brother, had wanted to get to know him and share a bond. They had a common enemy, their father, who considered both of them no good. And they had both been pawns in the war between Derek's parents.

But Ethan had chosen to remain at a distance—and to hate Derek with every fiber of his being, until Derek had no choice but to hate Ethan in return.

"I repeat," Derek said. "What are you doing here?"

Ethan propped a shoulder against a wood pillar and smiled sardonically. "You never change, do you, brother? You always think the world belongs to you and you alone. I hate to be the one to bring your glass house crashing down, but the rest of us have just as much right to be here as you. So you had best get used to it."

"The rest of the world can stay. You, however, can get the hell out."

"Tsk, tsk. That's not a very loving attitude. You know what Mother used to say: vengeance is best left to the Lord. You'd heed that advice if you know what's good for you—though you were never very good at that, were you?"

A familiar knot cramped Derek's jaw. "Mother? Certainly you're not referring to *my* mother? *Your* mother was a whore who chose to spread her thighs and then abandon you on my family."

The slight tensing of his half-brother's shoulders was the only outward sign that Derek had struck a nerve. Ethan had always been better at controlling his emotions, and that, perhaps more than anything else, stoked Derek's anger the most.

"How could I possibly forget?" Ethan replied with a mocking grin. "You and our dear father took every opportunity to remind me of my illegitimacy. But Lady Emmaline, bless her English heart, loved me like my own mother couldn't. She took me under her wing and nurtured me like a baby chick, and look at me now. Rather formidable, wouldn't you say? No longer the scruffy ragamuffin who could be bullied."

"Don't delude yourself. Under that refined accent and those refined clothes, you're still that skinny, dirty urchin who was dumped on our doorstep. And you were never bullied; you were always the instigator. Tormenting the children of the village, throwing rocks at the farmers, shooting the hens for the hell of it—and then there were all those 'accidents' I had, like the fall from my horse when I was fifteen that broke my leg, or the time I got locked in the vault. No one found me for three days. I could have died."

"Yet here you are, safe and sound, and unfortunately no better for your trials."

"No thanks to you," Derek bit out, his fists throbbing from clenching them so hard.

"So you've always said. You managed to turn the entire clan against me and have me sent off to America to live with Lady Emmaline's pious sister."

"That year without you was worth all the grief."

"I imagine you spent every waking moment praying my ship went down at sea."

Derek's life would have been so much easier if

Ethan had gone away and never returned. But no matter how much he'd hated his half-brother, he had never wished him dead.

"Why bother talking about what could have been?" Derek replied. "For some reason my mother left you a stipend. You're financially independent, so why don't you use your cache to disappear into the vast reaches of civilization? Perhaps explore the world of albino pygmies or travel to France and socialize with the other pompous asses."

Ethan tapped his forefinger against his chin. "While your suggestion sounds intriguing, there are two things stopping me. The first is that your dear mother didn't leave me all that much blunt. In the end she loved her own flesh and blood better, or she would have left me the estates."

"They go with the title," Derek reminded him stiffly.

"Which you shunned, to live among the Scots who will never fully accept you. No matter what you do, you will never be one of them, unlike me. My blood is pure. What a twist of fate that is."

Derek forced himself to loosen his fists. "And the second reason stopping you from disappearing?" he prompted.

"That should be readily apparent," Ethan said with a shrug. "I live to annoy you. Really, what other enjoyments do I have? Why deny myself life's simple pleasures?"

Derek took a step toward his brother, who matched the move, mere inches separating them. "I could permanently bar you from the clan."

"But you won't, because it would appear as though you couldn't handle me. Take heart, brother, there are other ways to be rid of me. You could throw me in a mask and shackle me in the dungeon, tell people I simply left one day, and you hadn't seen or heard from me since."

"Though," he went on with a smirk, "I doubt you'd be able to live with your conscience. That was always your problem, wasn't it? You were never able to let me get what I deserved, even when Father knew it had to be me who had nearly killed the heir apparent in the vault. You wouldn't let him beat me; you had to say that you might have accidentally locked yourself in, or that the wind could have blown the door shut."

Ethan shook his head and smiled benignly. "A conscience is clearly a burden, and I'm glad I don't have one. For no matter what it takes, I intend to show the clan that you are not who they think you are. My mission is to dethrone you—and I will, before too long."

Before Derek could lunge at his brother, a thick arm thrust between them. "Do y' lads never get enough of bein' at each other's throats?" Derek shot a glare at Darius, who shook his head in reproach before turning his regard on Ethan. "What is in ye boy, tae be harborin' so much anger and resentment toward the only remainin' family y've got? Derek isn't the one you should be spewin' y'r venom on."

"And who is, old man?" Ethan asked in a savage tone, a muscle working in his jaw. "You?"

"Nay, I'm a peace-lovin' soul, as y' well know. But this feuding between you and y'r brother—"

"Half-brother," Derek bit out. "And I have my doubts about that, considering his mother."

Ethan's hand shot toward Derek's throat, but Darius pushed him back. "Enough! Two grown men actin' like bairns." Darius threw up his hands and stepped out from between them. "You"—he pointed at Derek—"have someone who needs you right now. The wee lass has no one tae help her. If y're bound and determine tae kill him or get yourself killed, then so be it. But dunna say I didn't warn y'."

A slow smile spread over Ethan's face. "Speaking of the wee lass . . ." He pushed past Derek and strode to the stairs. "Good morning, Lady Rosalyn. I cannot say how pleased I am to see you again."

Derek spun around. Christ, he had forgotten about Rosalyn, and Ethan took full advantage, moving in on her like a shark, as he had done every time Derek was by her side in London. Then, as now, he switched off his smug attitude and turned on the charm.

Derek felt like doing bodily injury as Ethan lifted Rosalyn's hand and placed a kiss on the back, lingering far longer than was necessary, which, of course, was his intention.

"You are a fetching sight, my dear," Ethan said. "Let us have a look at you." He took her hand and drew her down the final step. "Lovely, as always."

"Thank you," she murmured, her gaze meeting Derek's, the concerned look in her eyes confirming that she had heard his run-in with his brother.

Tucking Rosalyn's hand in the crook of his arm, Ethan escorted her into the room. "What a wonderful surprise to see you. I was most unhappy when I learned of your departure from London. Lady Dane kept mum about your sudden leave-taking." Flashing a look at Derek, he said, "Now I see why.

"But," he continued in a light tone, "I've found you again, and I don't intend to let you out of my sight this time—we shall be boon companions. I know you love to ride, and if you'd like I'll let you take my mount, Sabbath. I'm sure he'll be quite happy to have you on top of him." Leaning close to her ear, he said loud enough for Derek to hear, "I know I would be."

Fury consumed Derek, and he slammed the heel of his hand into Ethan's chest, knocking him back. Pointing a finger in his face, Derek said through clenched teeth, "You are to stay away from her. Do you understand?"

Ethan straightened and dusted off his shoulder. "Are you proposing to tell me what to do? I think we've discovered that I'll do what I want."

"When I have you turned out, *then* we'll see what you'll do."

"My lord, please . . . ," Rosalyn beseeched, not wanting to be the cause of a problem. "I'm sure he meant no harm." The furious look Derek leveled on her warned her not to get involved.

Ethan's smile was a mere baring of teeth. "You heard the lady, brother. Be nice to me. I've had a difficult life, or hadn't you heard?"

"Enough, boy," Darius said warningly. "Be done with it."

"I haven't even started, uncle."

"Don't make me tell you again," Derek said in a taut voice. "You won't like the outcome."

"So you're finally shedding that yellow streak? Bravo, I never thought the day would come. Surely something is behind this amazing transformation. What might that be?"

Leaning forward, Ethan's warm breath fanned Rosalyn's cheek as he said, "I believe it's you, my lady. It seems you have brought about a miraculous change in the lad. King Manchester is known to have an icy heart that not even the equatorial sun can melt.

"Well, this will make for an intriguing stay. Now if you'll excuse me, Sabbath is waiting for me, and I'd like to let him know that he may have a visitor." With a devilish smile, Ethan inclined his head to Rosalyn. "Good day, my dear." Turning, he said with a mocking tone, "Always a delight, brother. And Darius, please stop hovering. You're like a pesky fly."

As Ethan left, Darius said, "If that boy wasn't half my age and twice my size, I'd kick him in the pants. Hard." He trudged out of the tavern, muttering something about seeing to the horses, which were in the traces and anxious to go.

Derek hesitated, then turned to face Rosalyn. In the muted light, she looked so young. Her hair had been brushed until it shone; a gleaming golden mass that he longed to run his fingers through.

He had only seen it down once, when he had barged into her room and discovered her bouncing on top of the steamer trunk.

Normally her hair was braided into a thick rope that hung down her back or else was looped upward and secured with combs, as it was this morning. The combs were a delicate pearl that matched the luster of her skin and the creamy color of her day dress.

"You look tired," he said, noting the dark circles under her eyes, which only made them look larger and more luminous. "Did you not sleep well?"

Her gaze dropped from his. "The accommodations were fine."

A moment of silence descended, then Derek said, "I'm sorry about what happened before. Ethan can be—"

She stopped him by laying her hand on his. "You need not explain. I have family that does not feel fondly toward me, either."

Without thought, Derek took both her hands in his and drew her toward him. The warm, sweet scent that rose from her skin made him ache to hold her. "I won't let anything happen to you."

"I know," she murmured. "But I can't help being frightened for you."

"Let me worry about myself. You just concentrate on relaxing. I can't say that Castle Gray can offer you as much entertainment as London, but I'll do my best."

"I was never overly fond of London. I always preferred the serenity of Cornwall, the long stretches of open spaces and the quiet beauty of the coast. Is Scotland like that?"

"In some regards. My home overlooks the ocean high atop a cliff, but it's far too dangerous for anyone to traverse, except those who know its perils."

"Like you."

He smiled. "Yes, I've been going up and down

those cliffs since I was in short pants. The landscape can seem harsh to some."

"But it's home to you, and that makes it special."

"I can't imagine living anywhere else."

"That's how I feel about Cornwall," she said wistfully.

Derek wanted to draw her into his arms and tell her that everything would be all right. "You're homesick."

"At times, I miss it terribly. Some of the best days of my life were spent wandering the beaches and exploring the coves with Fancy."

"Lady Francine, you mean?"

A smile filtered across Rosalyn's lips. "No one ever calls her Lady Francine. She's simply Fancy. She befriended me when I first came to Cornwall with my mother and stepfather. She's bright and fun and generous. I don't know what my life would have been like without her."

"I met her at Lady Dane's. She seemed . . . a handful."

Rosalyn's eyes twinkled. "That's Fancy. I don't know how Mr. Kendall will ever handle her. Fancy is not used to anyone telling her what to do. She's very independent."

Derek chuckled. "I sensed that. But I wouldn't worry about Lucien. He's been through battles with far fiercer combatants. I'm sure he can hold his own."

"I don't know. Fancy can be hardheaded—but never mean. She is the sweetest, most loving person I've ever known. Without a second thought, she risked her life and her home to take me in when Calder threatened me."

"She's a good friend."

"The very best," Rosalyn answered, pensively biting the edge of her lip.

"She'll be fine, Rosalyn. I know Lucien. He's a good man. Wherever they may be, Fancy is in capable hands."

"I know," she murmured. "And I must say, Mr. Kendall really has a great deal of fortitude."

"He definitely has that," Derek remarked, resisting the urge to laugh. Lucien would get a kick out of hearing Rosalyn's view of him. Of all the men in the Pleasure Seekers club, Lucien was the most mule-headed—fortitude was a nice way of putting it. "It sounds to me as though you admire your friend quite a bit."

"Oh, I do! Fancy's always been so strong. There

was nothing she couldn't do if she put her mind to it."

Derek stroked his thumb absently along Rosalyn's jaw. "You're just as strong, you know."

A flush stained her cheeks, and Rosalyn looked down at her hands, shaking her head. "That's very nice of you to say—"

Derek tipped her head up. "I don't say things just to be nice. Look how well you've held up with all the trouble your stepbrother has put you through." Her face fell, and Derek wanted to kick himself for reminding her.

"He'll never give up, you know. He's very tenacious," she said.

"That's fine, because I don't give up, either."

The way she looked into his eyes told Derek how very innocent she was, and he found himself taking a step closer, watching those beautiful eyes turn a darker shade of green, the urge to kiss her a growing hunger in his gut.

Her soft breath fanned his neck as she murmured, "Had you not come along when you did . . ."

Derek leaned down and pressed his forehead to hers. "But I did, and I'm very glad. I want you to feel welcome in my home. What's mine is yours." He lifted his head a fraction, his gaze centered on her lips, action following thought as his mouth descended toward hers.

"Good Lord, man." Darius's voice jarred them, making Derek want to wring his uncle's neck. "Are y' goin' tae kick around in here all day? We'll not make it for supper at this rate, and if I'm forced tae miss another of cook's meals, I'll be blamin' you."

Though his uncle's sudden intrusion was the cold water Derek needed to stop what he had almost done, he didn't feel one bloody bit relieved. Another moment, and he would have devoured Rosalyn.

Yet the more she trusted him, the less he could indulge in his attraction for her. He was her protector now—and yet, her biggest threat. Just taking her away could cause damage to her reputation, should anyone find out.

Cupping her elbow, Derek led Rosalyn from the tavern. A chill lingered in the air, but the bright morning sun would soon burn it away.

The journey would be less comfortable, as the terrain was rough in spots. He'd send Darius ahead to get things ready for Rosalyn's arrival; she would be exhausted by the time they got to his home.

Derek opened the coach door and handed Rosalyn in. In the doorway, she turned to look down at him.

"My lord, I never asked you if my coming to your home would cause any problems. Is there anyone who might be upset by my showing up with you?"

Derek could think of at least a dozen people, off the top of his head. To some, the English would always be the enemy. But he would deal with anyone who did not make her welcome—and it would not be pleasant.

"You have nothing to worry about. Everyone will adore you."

The smile that lit her face was all the reward he needed; he was determined to make everything right for her.

The only question was . . . how?

Six

Rosalyn found herself very conscious of Derek as the miles rolled away beneath the coach wheels.

He was a man of contradictions. He seemed so contained most of the time, yet at the tavern he had been so gentle, so tender. Rosalyn actually believed that he had been about to kiss her, and she would have welcomed it.

She was confused about her feelings. Though she desired Derek, getting her heart involved would only leave her hurt in the end—for she could never marry him.

A radical thought crept into her mind. Since she would never marry, perhaps she should consider being a paramour. She had never questioned her own passion, which was such a powerful part of her, and no man but Derek had ever stirred that passion.

But would he even want that?

She darted a glance at him. His head was tipped back and his eyes closed; in sleep, he looked even more handsome.

Rosalyn forced herself to look away and stop her scandalous flights of fancy. She studied her surroundings instead, becoming enchanted by the landscape passing the coach window.

The terrain was surprisingly lush and the grass verdant. Jagged peaks of rock forced their way out of the earth at odd intervals, but their rugged faces only added to the mysterious beauty.

She found many similarities between Scotland and Cornwall. Both had uncompromising elements and stark seascapes, intense loveliness and barren vistas. And both could be lonely and isolated to those who needed many people around them to feel comfortable.

Dark clouds had rolled in, the moisture-laden air heralding an unexpected shower. But the strong wind that blew off the Atlantic would clear the skies quickly to reveal the bright green moors and heather-covered plateaus.

Derek had told her that Castle Gray sat between two mountain ranges, the Northwest Highlands and the Grampian Hills. A valley called Glen More—or the Great Glen—divided the two. The highest mountains in the Highlands jutted along the Atlantic, with deep glens cut among the barren peaks, scattered trees, and evergreen scrub.

Derek's home sat on a plateau looking out toward the island of Mull, part of the Inner Hebrides, where large flocks of sheep grazed precariously close to the cliff's edge, protected only by the dogs trained to guard and herd them.

Rosalyn was looking forward to seeing it. But what she wanted even more was something she hadn't had in a long time: peace. Peace of heart and peace of mind. She had felt neither since her parents died.

A sudden jolt of the carriage nearly toppled her out of her seat. Two strong hands at her waist kept her upright, as Derek shot forward, coming awake instantly.

The coach listed to the left side, but its speed did not slow. She could hear the horses blowing hard, fear pushing them on to an even greater pace.

"What's happened?" she shouted over the shriek of splintering metal. As soon as the words were out of her mouth, a terrible thought occurred to her.

Calder.

Derek's grip tightened on her arms. "Stay calm. We'll be fine." He lifted her hand to a leather strap above the right-side door. "Hold this tightly. Do not let it go."

Rosalyn nodded and held the strap with a death grip as Derek slid to the opposite side and leaned his head out the window.

"The wheel's cracked," he said over the din. He threw back the panel behind the driver's box and shouted, "Get those damn horses under control."

"I'm tryin', m'lord," the driver bellowed. Rosalyn could hear the fright in his voice. "A piece of wood came up and hit the lead horse in his rear flank an' now he's wild."

Derek reached through the panel and took hold of the reins, muscles straining the seams of his jacket as he fought for control over the animals.

He let out a piercing whistle, one long burst and two short ones. Within moments the horses began to slow, and finally the coach clattered to a stop, the left side tilting precariously.

When Rosalyn dared to take a peek outside, her heart dropped to her stomach. They had come very close to running straight off a cliff.

She closed her eyes, thanking God and whatever powers had prevented all of their deaths. She started as a hand settled on her cheek. Her eyes snapped open to find Derek staring at her, concern on his face.

"Are you all right?"

Rosalyn blinked and sat up. "I'm fine. What happened?"

"It seems the wheel well split and then broke the wheel itself."

"How?"

"I'm not sure, but I intend to find the answer." He pressed his shoulder against the door, which stuck and then cracked open on its hinges, banging into the side of the coach. Derek jumped down and disappeared behind the boot.

Rosalyn could hear him talking with the driver. She slid across the seat and tried to catch what the men were saying. Only one word reached her.

Sabotage.

A shiver ran down her spine. It was Calder. It had to be. But how had he discovered her whereabouts so quickly? She had been so sure that she had covered her tracks well this time.

Rosalyn closed her eyes. She would never get away from him. He was a man determined. He would get her money no matter what he had to do. What if she just gave it to him? Perhaps he would leave her alone then.

Once again, she had succeeded in getting some-one else involved in her trouble. She couldn't live with herself if anything happened to Derek, which left her only one choice: she must leave.

Tonight, after everyone had gone to sleep, she would sneak out. She wouldn't allow herself to think about how forbidding the terrain might be. Nor did she concern herself with the fact that she didn't know where she would go.

All she knew was that she could no longer en-danger others to save herself. From here on, she would have to do this alone. But she must not let on to Derek that anything had changed. If he had even an inkling of what she was contem-plating, he would certainly stop her—though she suspected he was wishing he had never met her right now.

·   ·   ·

Derek was kicking himself for getting Rosalyn involved in his troubles when she had enough of her own.

He could tell that the break in the wheel well had been no accident. Someone had purposely caused the damage—and he was fairly certain he knew who.

Ethan.

There was no one else with either the motive or the opportunity. And no one else hated Derek as much as his half-brother. Ethan had been trying to do away with him since they were youths, and clearly he was still trying. Bastard.

"Say nothing of this," Derek told his driver firmly. "Do you understand?"

"Aye, y'r lordship. My lips are sealed."

"Good, now see if you can get this repaired. We're only a few miles from Castle Gray. I'll unhitch two of the horses to ride there, and send someone back to help."

"Aye, sir." Jessup hunkered down beside the wheel to begin repairs.

When Derek strode around the carriage to check on Rosalyn, he noticed a stiffness in her bearing. She must be frightened. He was, too, though for her rather than himself.

"Jessup is working on the problem," he told her. "Are you up for a ride? My home is only a few miles from here. We could be there before dusk and have you in a nice bath. Sound good?"

"It sounds very nice," she said, her voice restrained. "Thank you."

As Derek reached out to help her down, an emotion flashed in her eyes that was too fleeting for him to grasp.

"Are you sure everything is all right?"

"Yes."

Something was definitely bothering her, but Derek knew that pushing her would only backfire. She was a stubborn lass, full of an untapped fire that made him crazy with wanting her.

As her long, slim fingers clasped his tightly, he gave them a gentle squeeze. Remaining a gentleman was becoming damn difficult. The entire trip, he had found himself covertly studying her: the way her hair fell, the slight curve toward the ends, the different hues of gold; the shape of her lips, their fullness, how soft they looked; the upturn at the corners of her eyes that gave her an exotic appearance; and the aura of sinfulness that seemed to belie her outward innocence.

Inevitably, his gaze had moved lower. He was mesmerized by the rise and fall of her chest, the way each inhale lifted her breasts, making them swell ever so slightly over the top of her bodice. He'd realized then that he needed to find an outlet for his growing ardor.

His thoughts turned to Caroline Trainor, his housekeeper. They had been lovers on and off for the last five years, and had become friends. He confided things to her that he wouldn't to most people, knowing she would not repeat them.

Theirs had been a convenient arrangement, but he had found himself using it less and less lately, as he noticed that things had subtly changed. Somewhere along the way he had become something more to Caroline; she harbored feelings for him that he could not return.

He had not had the heart at first to tell her there was no future for them, but neither did he want her missing the opportunity for love with the right man. So he had finally told her they were over right before he left for London. They could still be friends, and he hoped that would not change, but there could be no more.

She had taken his news without crying or recriminations. Instead she had smiled and quietly left the room. He didn't know what to expect upon his arrival, but hoped it didn't include a weapon aimed at his privates.

"My lord?"

Derek realized that he was standing by the horses, but not unhitching them. He shook his head and turned to Rosalyn, who looked too damn tempting standing in a ray of waning sunlight.

"You can ride Gypsy," he said as he removed the harnesses. "She's more docile than Minotaur."

"Either will be fine. I've been riding since I was three."

Derek walked Gypsy over to her. "I guess what I should have said was that Gypsy prefers women riders. Can't say that I blame her." He handed Rosalyn the reins and smiled, heartened when she smiled back.

She rubbed the horse's nose. "Well, Gypsy, I guess it's you and me." Gypsy whinnied and bobbed her head. Rosalyn laughed, the musical sound enchanting Derek. Light danced in her eyes as she glanced up at him and said, "Shall we go?"

Derek had to mentally shake himself to break the spell of her smile. "Yes."

He cupped his hands and held them out to help her mount. Once she was comfortably settled, he swung up onto Minotaur. The horse pranced sideways, unused to having a rider on his back.

"Which way to your home?" Rosalyn asked.

Derek pointed toward the northeast. "Around that low ridge of mountains and straight on."

"All right then," she said with a laugh. "Last one there must brush down the other's horse."

She gave Gypsy a nudge in the flanks and shot off. Derek wheeled Minotaur around and took after her.

He marveled at how expertly she handled her mount, though his heart nearly stopped when she coaxed the horse into jumping a wide length of scrub brush, easily making it to the other side.

He could hear her laughter as he thundered up behind her. Her hair had pulled free of the few pins that had held it in its stylish arrangement. Now it rippled down her back like a banner of silken sunlight, tendrils whipping against her face as she turned to find him gaining on her.

She urged her horse on and Derek called out to her to slow down, but she could not hear him over the sound of her horse's galloping hooves.

He prodded Minotaur, but the stallion was not as young as Gypsy and could not maintain the pace. Rosalyn drew farther ahead, and then the sound of her scream tore through him. Gypsy's back leg had tangled in some low-lying vines, bringing the horse down to her front knees and sending Rosalyn flying over her head. Derek lost sight of her for a moment, then saw her lying in a thatch of heather.

He jumped from Minotaur's back before the horse had come to a stop and ran to Rosalyn's side, gently cradling her head in his hands. "Rosalyn?"

She moaned and stirred slightly before finally blinking open her eyes, trying to focus. "What happened?"

"You took a tumble from your horse. How do you feel?"

She moved a bit and winced. "Like a discarded sack of potatoes." She endeavored to smile, the sight draining Derek's fear.

She slowly sat up, and Derek put his arm beneath her back, then carefully shifted her into his lap, her head cradled against his shoulder. "Better?"

"Yes," she murmured. "You needn't worry."

"Do you ache anywhere?"

Rosalyn ached all over, but she did not want to tell him so. Her own foolishness had caused her accident. If she had not been acting like a silly child, none of this would have happened. "Is Gypsy all right?"

"Gypsy is fine. She's got a bit of a kink in her right leg, but she'll work that out in a few days."

"I'm sorry," she said.

"Ssh," Derek soothed, brushing stray tendrils from her face and stroking his fingers through her long hair.

"I was reckless."

"You were enjoying yourself. I should have warned you how unpredictable the landscape can be. One moment it's flat, and the next, dips appear. You'll have to ride double with me the rest of the way. You don't mind, do you?"

"No." While she regretted what had happened, she couldn't regret the outcome. She wanted to be held in Derek's arms. She had not felt them around her since the night of the Senhavens' rout, when he had pushed his way through the circle of men around her and held out his hand, a silent request for a dance. Without a word, Rosalyn had taken his hand and been swept away. She had felt like a fairy princess that night.

As though she were made of glass, Derek helped her to her feet. When she stood before him, the world around them seemed to melt away. As though he had read her thoughts and knew what she wanted most at that moment, he leaned down and brushed a kiss across her lips.

He eased away and Rosalyn moaned in protest, not wanting the moment to end. He needed no further incentive, pulling her tight against his chest.

He deepened the kiss, his tongue darting into her mouth to mate with hers, tasting her; his hand cupping the back of her head, keeping her close, as though he thought she would run away. But that was the last thing on Rosalyn's mind as she twined her fingers through his hair.

His other hand moved against her waist, squeezing lightly and then shifting restlessly up and down her side until finally settling on the outer swell of her breast, the image that had kept her tossing and turning in her bed every night, waiting for his hand to slip across her silken skin and lightly caress her nipples.

"Derek," she whispered in an aching voice as his lips feverishly skimmed her jaw and moved down her neck, the sensations arrowing straight to the core of her.

She arched up on her toes and followed his lead, pressing her lips to his neck, reveling in his husky groan and growing bolder by the moment. She shifted so that his hand fully covered her breast, her nipple peaking against her bodice and into his palm.

The next moment, he pulled away.

She reached for him, but he stepped back. "That shouldn't have happened."

Why?

He glanced away, looking toward the setting sun. "We must go or we'll be stuck out here in the dark."

Rosalyn knew he was doing what he thought was best for both of them. And she shouldn't want him to kiss her again. But she did, and the more he made her yearn for him, the more she thought being a mistress might not be so terrible.

Her reputation would be ruined, should anyone find out. But what did it matter? She would never be a wife, and too much passion existed inside her to consider a life in a convent or spinster-hood. Derek had made her see that she wanted to be a woman in the most complete way.

"Take my hand," he said, and Rosalyn glanced up to find him astride Minotaur's back, looking down at her, his face devoid of any expression.

She raised her hand to his, and in a moment she was seated across his lap, his body tense beneath hers.

They rode in silence for a long time. Rosalyn tried to remain stiff in his arms, when she really wanted to lay her head against his shoulder and close her eyes.

"Did you get your mother's estate settled?" she asked when she could no longer take the silence.

"Yes," he said. "I transferred ownership of all but one estate to the charge of my mother's last remaining brother."

"You didn't want them?"

"I have more than I need here."

"But you didn't renounce your title."

"It would have broken my mother's heart. I am, after all, part English. That's not something I can change."

"Would you, if it were possible?"

He was quiet for so long that Rosalyn thought that she had insulted him. But finally he spoke.

"There were times when I thought I would, when I believed it would be simpler to not be of mixed descent—tainted blood, as many people around here look at it. But it was as much my mother as my father that made me who I am. There aren't many people who can travel between two different worlds. Some look at me as though I'm a heathen, while others see me as a sophisticated gentleman."

"And which do you believe yourself to be?"

"A bit of both, though I'm not expected to be so perfect here as I am in England. Besides, I'm needed more here. The title and estates will take care of themselves."

"It's important for you to be needed." She knew it to be true. He was a man of honor and strength, a leader in every sense of the word.

She could see the fire burning in his eyes, a passion for the country he called home. "Being needed is what brings meaning to life. Don't you want to be needed?"

"Of course."

"So tell me, what brings meaning to your life?"

She glanced out over the moors to the distant

promontories, whose massive height and width held the pounding sea at bay.

"Back in Cornwall, there was a small orphanage run by the local parish. The priest only had the help of two nuns, neither in the bloom of youth, and the children were quite the imps. I spent many hours playing with them."

"Do you want to have children someday?"

A familiar yearning rose inside her, but she immediately quelled it. "I decided a long time ago that there are enough children in this world who need love and attention, and I'd like to devote my time to them."

"You wouldn't want babies of your own to nurture?"

Rosalyn heard the surprise in Derek's tone. She knew her desire not to have children had to seem odd. But that possibility had died years ago, and she refused to allow the hurt to rule her life.

"I don't need children of my own to feel fulfilled. I'm happy to help others."

Derek regarded Rosalyn's profile when she looked away. He had never imagined her as a woman who didn't want children. She had such a gentle way about her. It didn't make sense.

Her sudden gasp brought his gaze to where her attention was focused. Over the crest of a hill, Castle Gray came into view.

"Oh my, is that your home?"

"Yes."

"I never imagined it would be so big! Is that a moat?"

"Yes, but the crocodiles were removed a decade ago."

She stared at him, wide-eyed. "Crocodiles?"

He laughed at her expression. "Welcome to Castle Gray, my lady."

Seven

❧

"She's more than five hundred years old, built by Saxon ancestors," Derek recited with pride, giving Rosalyn some of the history of his home as they rode along. "The upper walkway has a completely circular view so enemies could be spotted either by land or sea. She's fully fortified with two drawbridges, eight guard stations equipped with cannonades, six turrets perfect for locking in damsels in distress, and one fully functional dungeon for the occasional torture." When Rosalyn's gaze snapped to his, Derek laughed. "No one's ever been tortured—at least not since I've been laird."

"You're incorrigible."

"So I've been told." He grinned. "But to continue, the majority of the village resides within the castle walls. The hawkers sell everything from fresh fish to lumber to oriental silk. In short, we are a city unto ourselves."

"Amazing."

"Yes," Derek agreed, watching the evening light casting red and gold prisms over the limestone walls. A familiar feeling of peace came over him.

Rosalyn looked at him. "It really is lovely," she said, laying her hand on top of his. "Thank you for inviting me here."

Without thought, Derek caressed her cheek. "You've already thanked me."

"I know." She glanced down at her hand entwined with his, aching to know how it would feel covering her breast. "But I wanted to tell you again."

Something about her demeanor unsettled Derek. Something was going on inside her head, but he couldn't put his finger on it. It would have been so much easier, had they met under different circumstances. Perhaps then he could indulge in his growing desire for her. The pressure of her soft bottom against his groin was nearly unbearable. He longed to raise her skirts from behind and ease into her, then thrust to the hilt and let her sweet, tight heat clutch him; to feel her tighten; her frenzy making him harden further, pump faster, rocking inside her until he felt her climax around him.

Derek clenched his hands and thanked the powers above that his long jacket hid his arousal.

He could only hope that now that he was home, he could stay away from her. He'd sent Darius ahead to have his staff prepare her a room in the west wing. His own suite of rooms was in the east wing. His men at arms resided in the middle. Not even a mouse could get by them, so there was no need for his room and Rosalyn's to be close to one another to ensure her safety. Only disaster would come of that arrangement, anyway. Derek doubted he would have the strength to deny himself if she was too close.

As it was, he could barely keep his hands off her. She felt so good in his arms. And the way she looked at him, with complete trust, was a heady feeling.

He couldn't let her down. He had already engaged a league of Bow Street runners in the pursuit of her stepbrother.

As well, his fellow Pleasure Seekers had gotten wind of Derek's plight and were keeping an eye out for Westcott. Even Lucien, with his own troubles, had forwarded a missive to offer his support. Derek knew his friend had his own concerns to deal with. But for the first time since Derek had learned of Lucien's problem, he felt that Lucien might finally fight his way free, with Fancy's help.

"My lord!" a voice rang out.

Derek looked toward the drawbridge to see Nathaniel running toward him. Caroline's son was nearing eight and full of hero-worship. He had never known his father. Derek had taken to guiding him in swordplay at Caroline's request, as her son was becoming too solitary, spending hours with his pigeons instead of with the other boys of the village.

While Derek had grown very fond of the lad, he was concerned that Nate was becoming too attached. Yet the youngster needed a man to guide him. If Derek had been able to get a name out of Caroline, he would have tracked down the miscreant who sired the boy.

Nate dashed up to the horse, his eyes bright and his face flushed from exertion. His mop of reddish brown hair was an unruly mess, making the lad look like a ragamuffin. He eagerly took the horse's reins. "Welcome home, sir!"

Derek leaned over and ruffled the boy's hair. "Thank you, Nate. It's good to be home. Has all been well here?"

"Aye, sir—well, all except Janie."

"And what has she done this time?"

"She let all the hens out of the henhouse, and I had to chase them down. I got bit by Belinda. See?" He raised his hand to show Derek a small peck mark.

"Who's Belinda?" Rosalyn asked.

"Belinda is a very big hen," Derek explained. "She rules the roost and has an infinitely short temper."

"I thought the rooster ruled the roost?"

"Normally that would be true. But you don't know Henry."

"Henry? That's the rooster's name?"

Derek grinned. "Not my choice, but it stuck."

"I think he's not right in the noggin,'" Nathaniel said, crossing his eyes. "One of the horses kicked him in the head, y' see. Never been the same since."

"Maybe a new rooster would make a difference," Rosalyn remarked.

"Oh, no, miss," Nathaniel piped in. "That won't do it. The hens around here aren't like any others."

"Neither are the women of the village," Derek said with a grin.

"Aye," the lad agreed with a pronounced nod. "They're real tough, and they look at their men all pinch-faced—like this." He scrunched his cheeks together, and Rosalyn laughed. "The men are always groanin' and hidin' out in the back barn."

"What are they doing in the back barn?" she asked curiously.

Nate shrugged. "Playing cards, mostly, and complaining about stuff. But ye know what?" he went on in a conspiratorial tone, lowering his voice.

Rosalyn leaned down and played her role. "What?"

"I think they like their women more than they let on. I see 'em huggin' an' kissin' each other when no one's lookin'." He made a face, and Rosalyn smiled.

Derek laughed. "You are going to get a bad reputation, lad. No one wants a Peeping Tom about."

"I'm not peeping, sir. They do it right in broad

daylight. Yuck! Who wants to kiss a girl? I'd rather kiss a toad."

"I guarantee that will change someday, my boy. And you'll find yourself wanting to kiss females a whole lot. Maybe even one in particular," he added, capturing Rosalyn's gaze.

He cleared his throat and turned to the boy.

"See to Gypsy, will you, Nate? And have Liam apply a poultice to her leg and keep her hobbled for the night."

"Aye, sir. Right away." He gently took hold of Gypsy's reins, speaking softly to her as he led her toward the stables.

"He's a darling boy," Rosalyn said.

"Yes, he's a good lad. He's desperate for a father, though."

"And he wants you to be that father, I imagine." She had no doubt that Derek would make a very good father.

"I think he'd prefer his own."

"I can understand that. My father died when I was six, and I longed for him. Even now, I miss him. Some days it's a struggle to recall what he looked like, but I remember that he always smelled like tobacco." She smiled to herself. "He loved a good pipe."

"At least you got to know your father for a short time."

"Yes. But what I remember most was how sad my mother was when he died. She told me Papa had gone to heaven. I asked her if I could go, too. She cried and hugged me close and told me heaven was a long way off. I didn't want it to be, I wanted to see my father again. Then my mother met Lord Westcott, and some of the happiness returned to her eyes. I wanted that for her. She deserved it."

"And what about you? Were you happy?"

Rosalyn nodded. "The earl was very good to me; he treated me like a daughter. He always told me he'd wished he had been blessed with a girl. His wife died shortly after Calder was born. He was devastated for many years. But he said that the sunshine came back to his life when he met my mother. They were good for each other. I don't think the earl wanted to live after my mother died." She gazed up at Derek. "I believe one can die of a broken heart. Don't you?"

Derek had never felt that measure of despair, but looking at Rosalyn, he knew how he would feel if anything happened to her.

"Yes, I do."

Minotaur plodded up to the stable doors, and Derek jumped down from his back. He held his hands up for Rosalyn, and she slid into his arms.

"When did you stop believing your father was coming back?" he asked.

She glanced over his shoulder, trying to hold back the tears that suddenly welled in her eyes. "When Calder told me he was dead and buried and that no one ever came back."

Damn the bastard for breaking a little girl's heart.

Derek handed Minotaur's reins to Nathaniel and patted the boy on the back. "Give him a good rubdown."

"Aye, sir."

Rosalyn watched the pair amble away. "Will Gypsy be all right?"

"Gypsy will be fine. Let's worry about you for now." Before Rosalyn knew what he intended, Derek lifted her into his arms.

"What are you doing?"

"It would appear I'm carrying you."

"I can walk."

"Consider me your personal cart horse."

"But—"

"Ssh."

Rosalyn closed her mouth at the look Derek leveled on her and resigned herself to her fate, knowing she was exactly where she wanted to be. When she was with him, her whole body vibrated with a voluptuous excitement.

As she rode on his lap, she had noted a suspicious bulge in his trousers, and wondered if she had been the cause. She'd barely resisted the urge to reach down and feel his hardness, to undo his buttons and take him into her hands.

Rosalyn forced her thoughts back to the moment. "Who's Janie?" she asked as Derek carried her across the inner bailey.

"She's the cook's daughter, and the cutest little sprite I've ever met. She's seven years old and fancies herself in love with Nathaniel"

"How sweet."

"Not for Nate." Derek chuckled, thinking about the turnaround the lad would someday go through in relation to women. "He thinks Janie is a pain in the rump, in his words. She follows him wherever he goes and makes bat eyes at him."

Before Rosalyn could reply, a voice called out, "Ah, brother, returned so soon?"

The smile faded from Derek's face upon spotting Ethan standing in the front doorway, leaning negligently against the frame.

Ethan focused on Rosalyn. "Have you made the biggest mistake of your life, my lady?"

Rosalyn stared at him, confused. Then it dawned on her that it might look as though Derek was carrying his wife over the threshold. "I hurt myself riding. Derek is being gallant."

Ethan let out a mocking laugh. "Well, that would undoubtedly be a first."

"It's none of your damn business what happened," Derek growled. "Now get out of the way before I knock your ass to the ground."

"Tsk, brother. Is that any way to speak in front of a lady? Besides, if I recall our last little brawl, I bloodied your face quite nicely."

"You punched me when I wasn't looking, you weasel. Now stand aside."

Ethan straightened abruptly, and Rosalyn feared the men would come to blows. "Oh!" she said with a moan, laying a hand across her stomach, hoping her act worked.

Derek immediately turned to her. "What's the matter? Are you ill?"

"I'm feeling dizzy. Might I lie down?"

"Certainly."

Derek brushed by Ethan. Rosalyn had a quick view of the beauty of the foyer, with its high-domed ceiling and magnificent Flemish tapestries on the walls.

From the front doorway, Ethan called, "Well done, my lady. But perhaps next time you should cradle your head if you feel dizzy. My darling brother is too enamored to notice, but I say bravo." He winked and disappeared out the door.

"Cretin," Derek muttered as he carried her down a long corridor where swords and battle-axes and battered old shields held evidence of darker years.

At the end of the hallway, Rosalyn spotted a doorway opened a crack. Derek stopped in front of it and shoved it open with his foot.

A startled gasp sounded from the corner of the room. When Derek entered, Rosalyn saw a lovely young woman.

Her hair was dark as midnight and spilled in soft waves to the middle of her back. The sleek tresses were held in place by a simple blue ribbon that matched her dress, which was worn in spots yet still flattered her figure.

"My lord," the woman said, holding a rag in one hand. "I had not heard you had returned. Welcome home."

"Thank you, Caroline. May I introduce you to Lady Rosalyn, who will be staying with us for a while. I hope you'll make her feel at home."

"Of course, m' lord." Yet when the woman's gaze settled on her, Rosalyn felt as though her presence was not wanted. "Welcome tae Castle Gray, my lady," she murmured, sketching a curtsey. "I hope ye enjoy y'r stay with us."

"Thank you, I'm sure I will."

Returning her attention to Derek, Caroline said, "I was just airing out her ladyship's room. Will there be anything else y'll be needin'?"

"A bath," Derek replied. "Lady Rosalyn has had a long trip. I'll also need Cyril to fetch Dr. Latham; our guest has taken a fall."

Cool amber eyes flicked to Rosalyn. "Y've been hurt, ma'am?"

"Hardly." Looking up at Derek, Rosalyn said, "I don't need a doctor."

"I'll let Latham decide. For now, let's get you into bed." Rosalyn could feel Caroline's eyes on her as Derek lifted the coverlet and slid her beneath it.

"This is unnecessary," she told him, uncomfortable with his coddling. "I'm fine now." Her protest went unheeded as Derek tucked her in.

Turning to Caroline, he said, "I want you to make sure she stays in bed until her bath arrives." He headed for the door. On the threshold he ordered, "Do not move from that spot. I'll be back to check on you."

Then he was gone.

Eight

$\mathscr{A}$ deafening silence descended as the door clicked shut.

Rosalyn shifted against the mound of pillows Derek had arranged behind her back and tried to think of something to say to his housekeeper.

She suspected that Caroline kept more than just Derek's house; she had seen that possessive light in a woman's eyes before. She knew the signs of love.

If Derek was having an affair with the woman, Rosalyn could only imagine how her presence made Caroline feel. She sought to reassure her, but wasn't certain she could. After all, whether she liked it or not, she was attracted to him herself.

"Y're English," the woman said bluntly, whether recrimination or simple observation Rosalyn could not discern.

"Yes, but I consider Cornwall my home."

"There isn't a place on the earth quite like Scotland," Caroline stated with pride.

"I'm beginning to agree with you."

Rosalyn hadn't forgotten her vow to leave tonight after everyone was in bed. She could only hope to get a good start on Derek. She wasn't foolish enough to believe he wouldn't come after her.

She had to get well out of the vicinity so that he would abandon his pursuit. She would leave him a note explaining what had prompted her departure.

Even as she sat there, Calder could very well be stalking Castle Gray's perimeter. Derek might believe his fortress secure, but Calder was wily. He would find a chink somewhere and slip in undetected. Rosalyn shivered.

"Are ye feelin' unwell, miss?"

"No," she lied. "Just eager to get up. Will you tell on me if I do?"

Her coconspirator nibbled her lip. "I suppose 'twill be all right. But his lordship does get mightily put out when his orders aren't obeyed."

Rosalyn smiled and tossed back the bedcovers. "I won't tell if you don't." She rose tentatively, testing her weight on her legs. Though one of her ankles felt a bit swollen and sore, and her back ached somewhat, she felt well overall. She took a few steps and stopped by the bedpost to admire a picture on the wall. "Who's that?"

"Oh, that's his lordship's mother, Lady Emmaline. She died a few months back." The housekeeper sighed and shook her head. "Tragic."

Rosalyn turned to her. "Why?"

Caroline hesitated, plucking at her skirt. "I imagine I shouldn't be sayin' anything . . ."

Rosalyn's curiosity was piqued. She hadn't been able to obtain any information about Derek except for what he himself had told her. People seemed to know very little about him and his life.

"Please say what you want," Rosalyn urged the young woman. "We are bound by a vow of silence, remember? Anything said here stays here."

"Aye, we are bound." She moved closer, peeking quickly at the door. Rosalyn followed her gaze, finding the secrecy all very dramatic.

The telling of tales seemed to abound in Derek's home. First Nathaniel, now Caroline. Castle Gray appeared a gossip's haven—not that Rosalyn had ever been a gossipmonger, but she burned to know more about Derek.

Perhaps he would prefer to tell her about his life himself rather than having it bandied about by servants? But while Rosalyn debated with her conscience, the opportunity to halt Caroline came and went.

"Well," the woman began in a lowered voice, leaning close, "perhaps tragic weren't the word I was lookin' for. Sad is perhaps more right. Two people never seemed more in love as the laird's mother and father, but never were two more wrong for one another."

"Why?"

"The old laird's father—Derek's grandfather—didn't want his son tae marry an Englishwoman. He had been around long enough tae remember the queen's oppression of the Scots. But the old laird, he was determined. He wanted the fair-haired English lass with her dainty ways and fancy dressin'. Guess he thought havin' her on his arm would make him more acceptable tae those high and mighty English folk with their noses up in the air. But it never did."

She shook her head sadly. "'Twas a shame tae see the missus so down about it. Those very same snooty folk shunned her, too, after she married a lowly Scotsman, no matter that he was laird. A heathen was a heathen, they said."

That was the label Derek had used, and the more Rosalyn heard it, the more she disliked it. As refined as Derek was, it was hard to believe that there were people who considered his blood tainted. He seemed far more a gentleman than many of the Englishmen she had met in London.

Even so, it was clear that he enjoyed more acceptance than his father did. Times had changed, though not as much as Rosalyn had thought.

"So what became of the relationship between Derek's parents?" Rosalyn asked.

Caroline sighed. "'Twas no surprise that it faltered and eventually broke apart. It didn't help when Master Ethan showed up on the doorstep, claimin' tae be the old laird's bastard, and there bein' those affirmin' it. That was the last straw for Lady Emmaline. Me, I was never quite sure. His lordship's father had himself a wanderin' eye, but he seemed tae love his wife. At least until she left him tae go back tae England.

"How his pride was torn," Caroline went on dramatically. "He vowed he'd never go after her, and he never did. But he wasn't the same after she left. It was strange, y' know? There had been many silences between the old laird and his lady, but when she was gone the silence was . . ." She frowned, searching for the word.

"Deafening?" Rosalyn supplied, understanding the depth of such silence after her mother died.

Caroline nodded. "Aye. I've never known the like. Poor Derek." A flush heated her cheeks as she flashed a quick glance at Rosalyn and hasten to correct, "I mean, his lordship. He got the brunt of the earl's sour disposition. The man looked at his son as though everything was his fault. Right in front of the lad, he would treat Master Ethan so much better, even though he hated that boy with a passion. It were the damnedest thing. One was the true heir and the other a bastard, but the roles seemed reversed. Do ye know what I mean?"

"Yes," Rosalyn murmured. "I do." She could see it all so clearly, and she better understood the depths of anger and bitterness between the brothers.

"Well, that's why Lord Derek won't marry himself an Englishwoman. Too many bad memories associated with his father's doomed marriage."

The housekeeper's revelation took Rosalyn a moment to digest. She noted the calculated look in the woman's eyes, as though everything she had imparted was meant to tell Rosalyn that Derek would never be interested in her due to her English roots.

"I see," Rosalyn said thoughtfully.

"As do I," a deep voice intoned, bringing Rosalyn whirling around to find Derek framed in the doorway, Darius standing a few feet behind him with one of her trunks. Derek stepped into the room, his gaze never wavering from hers as he said, "I hope this little tête-à-tête has been edifying for the both of you."

Rosalyn felt ashamed; it wasn't right to talk about him beneath his very roof. He stopped her apology with a raised hand.

"See to your duties, Caroline," he said gruffly, scowling as she hurried past him into the hallway. Returning his attention to Rosalyn, he said, "Where would you like your trunks?"

Rosalyn pointed to the far corner. "There is fine. Thank you."

Darius entered with one trunk, Nathaniel lugging the other. The boy regarded her with worried brown eyes; he clearly thought she was in dire trouble.

Darius shook his head but left without uttering a single word. Nathaniel lingered, obviously disinclined to leave. "Should I be fetchin' anything for the lady, sir?" he asked Derek, who had yet to redirect his penetrating stare from her.

"No. That will be all."

"But what about the miss's bath?"

As though on cue, the copper tub arrived, followed by several servants carrying steaming buckets of hot water, then several more carrying pails of cold, until the tub was filled to capacity and looked ever so inviting. All she wanted to do was soak for an hour; her limbs were beginning to ache.

But Rosalyn doubted she would be given much time to enjoy the bath; it appeared she was in for a lecture.

"Perhaps the miss would like some food?" Nathaniel persisted, looking hopefully at Derek.

"Nothing is going to happen to Lady Rosalyn, lad, so you needn't worry."

"Oh, I wasn't worryin', sir," Nathaniel said in a rush, dismissing the possibility that he wasn't absolutely confident of his hero's intentions. "I know ye'd never hurt a fly and that ye just like tae look mean when y're really not."

Derek cocked a brow. "I'm not?"

Rosalyn saw the hint of a smile as Derek folded his arms across his chest. A rather impressive chest, as she had noticed far too often for her peace of mind.

"Naw," Nathaniel replied. "Ye just like tae huff a lot."

Rosalyn put a hand over her mouth to cover her laugh.

"Ye'd never hurt no one—not unless ye had tae. But ye'd never harm a lady, 'specially one as pretty as the missus." To Rosalyn, the young boy said, "He thinks y're pretty, miss. He looks at ye all funny, like how Janie looks at me." He grimaced at the reminder of his unwanted sweetheart.

"You're a fine man, Nathaniel," Rosalyn told him. "Someday you'll make some lucky girl very happy."

He tilted his head questioningly. "How am I going tae make her happy?"

"Never mind," Derek answered, taking hold of the boy's thin shoulders and turning him toward the door. "Now out with you. You've said enough for one day."

"All right, I'll go. But if ye need me, miss, I'll be in the stables." He started toward the door and then turned halfway around. "I just thought the lady should know that ye don't bite, is all. She looks kinda worried and I don't think that's right, what with her bein' injured and all. Do you think that's right, sir?"

"Point taken," Derek conceded. "The lady will be pampered until she's well again. Does that ease your mind?"

Nathaniel beamed. "Aye, sir." Shifting his gaze to Rosalyn, he said, "Bye, miss. Y'll be fine now. His lordship always keeps his word." With that pronouncement, he skipped off—and Rosalyn found herself alone with Derek.

He reached back and pushed the door closed, making Rosalyn very much aware of an expanding ache within her that fanned to life every time she was with Derek.

Her mind whirred with her hidden fantasies, imagining Derek taking her down onto the bed, stripping her bare and wetting her skin with his lips and tongue, bringing her to the brink before he slid up and entered her without a word.

"I think young Nathaniel is smitten with you," Derek said, bringing her back to the present as he took a few leisurely steps toward the tub, where steam evaporated into the air.

Rosalyn struggled for breath. "He's a sweet boy."

Derek nodded, running the tips of his fingers across the surface of the water, making Rosalyn wish it was her skin instead. "You do have a way of affecting males of all ages."

"I hadn't noticed."

"You don't, do you?" He slowly moved toward her, a sensual rhythm in each step, leaving Rosalyn feeling trapped as he came to a stop in front of her. "If you'd like to know anything about me, all you have to do is ask. If I feel it's something you should know, then I'll give you my best answer."

His nearness was unnerving, and Rosalyn sought a breath to quiet her pounding pulse. "I wasn't prying. It was just that I noticed the painting." She pointed to it, needing a diversion. "Your mother was very lovely."

Derek regarded the portrait. "Yes, she prided herself on her appearance. I remember when she sat for the artist. My father had just given her that necklace."

Rosalyn had noted the magnificent emerald and diamond necklace dangling in the hollow of his mother's throat. "It's beautiful."

"A family heirloom. My mother insisted she be buried in it. It was more a symbol of triumph than a treasured item of jewelry. It was the final peace offering my father endeavored to make with my mother. Unfortunately, it was shortly before Ethan arrived. That's an entirely different sordid tale, though I suspect you've gotten an earful."

"I heard some of the story, but I'd rather hear it from you."

He absently swept a lock of hair off her shoulder. "That, my dear, is a long and boring tale, best left for old age. Right now, your bath is growing cold. Do you need any help undressing?"

That was the second time he had asked, and if he asked a third time, she very well might give in to temptation. "No, I'm sure I can manage."

"So I assume the buttons at the back of your gown open on command, then?"

Rosalyn had figured she could undo some and pull the dress over her head. Though she would have preferred his assistance, having him so close and feeling his fingers skimming her skin would be more than she could bear.

"Perhaps you could send a maid?"

"Certainly," he returned. "But I'm here now, and I have two hands. You'll find that we don't stand much on formality around here. So if you trust me to undo a few buttons with the promise that I'm harboring no ulterior motives, I'd be more than willing to help."

Rosalyn knew when she was cornered. If she said no, it would appear as though she didn't trust him, when it was herself she didn't trust. "I would be grateful for your assistance."

Rosalyn closed her eyes as Derek leisurely undid one button after the next, a shiver running through her body as his fingers lightly grazed her skin, each whispering caress feeling deliberate rather than accidental.

She barely noticed when the sleeves of her dress slipped off her shoulders, or when Derek's hands stopped moving and settled on her waist to turn her around.

His voice was a dark whisper as he said, "You're free."

"Thank you," she murmured, gazing in the deep blue eyes studying her so intensely.

"You're welcome." He glanced down at her lips, and Rosalyn felt them tingle in anticipation. "Perhaps I should stay and make sure you don't have any trouble getting in and out of the tub? I promise to keep my eyes closed."

She would have preferred he join her in the warm, silky water and the thought danced through her head of whispering an indecent invitation. He would respond with a low growl of anticipation as he quickly divested himself of his clothes and lifted her into his arms and into the water. He would turn her toward him and oh-so-expertly guide her onto his shaft, easing her down by her hips and slowly back up.

For long moments, no sound would be heard but his heavy breathing and the lapping of water around their entwined bodies. She would open to him, bring him in deep to the hilt and sink down again, her flesh quivering with pleasure, the ride slow and torturous until spasms pulsed around him, tightening in delicious torrents until he tipped his head back and groaned.

"Thank you for the offer," she murmured breathlessly, "but I'm sure I'll be fine."

A roguish half-grin lifted the corner of his lips. "Do you realize how much time we spend thanking each other?"

Rosalyn couldn't help a smile of her own. "Quite a bit, I believe."

"One might think we're avoiding something else."

"Like what?" But she knew. The sexual connection between them had been flame-hot from the start.

"I can think of any number of things, none of which I feel inclined to discuss just now," he replied in a husky tone.

Rosalyn's heart skipped a beat at the look in his eyes and her breathing grew shallow as he drew nearer. "Perhaps I should take my bath."

Derek wrapped an arm around her waist and pulled her tight against his chest. "I know I said I wouldn't do this again," he groaned against her lips, "but I can't seem to help myself."

His mouth settled over hers, gently at first, but becoming more demanding. He was insistent, and her hands instinctively lifted to his shoulders to grip the hard band of muscle and hold on for dear life.

Her dress slid unheeded to puddle at her feet. Derek kicked it away and lifted her snug against his body, so that all she could feel and taste was him.

Rosalyn whimpered as his mouth plundered hers. He was a hot, hard brand, burning her with his heat. She felt ravaged and desirable and on fire—and she didn't want him to stop.

She grasped fistfuls of his shirt as his lips and tongue moved down her throat, sending swirls of sensation to the pit of her belly. She had never experienced anything like this.

Then she was tumbling back, falling onto the soft bed as Derek sprawled on top of her, pinning her there with his weight, heavy and divine.

She twined her fingers in his silky hair, gripping the coal black strands as he feathered kisses down to the soft swells of her breasts. Her skin was covered by nothing more than her shift, a single pink ribbon the only barrier between his seeking mouth and her swollen nipples.

Her entire body pulsated with excitement, the sensations rising to a boiling point as his mouth moved down her neck, along her collarbone . . . and down the cleft between her breasts.

"Derek," she moaned, knowing with that single utterance what she was asking for. She didn't care.

Her plea seemed to throw cold water on his ardor, as he suddenly stopped and looked down at her. "Jesus," he muttered, closing his eyes.

Rosalyn cupped his cheek, feeling the tickle of his whiskers. She tried to make him look at her, but he wouldn't. Instead he rolled off her and lay beside her on the bed, staring at the canopy above their heads.

He was silent for long moments before finally saying, "The blame is entirely mine. I said this wouldn't happen again, and it appears I am a liar. I want to tell you this is the last time, but Christ . . . I can't be sure."

His gaze slid to hers. "The plain fact is, I want you. Perhaps my motives weren't as altruistic as I believed them to be when I came to your aid in London."

He shook his head and sat up. "I'll understand if you want to leave. I can make arrangements in the morning. Perhaps that's what I should have done from the start." As he stood up Rosalyn reached for him, but he stepped away. "I'll send Caroline up in an hour for your decision." Then he left, the door closing quietly behind him.

Rosalyn laid back down and hugged herself. She was as much to blame as Derek believed himself to be. She should have sent him away when he offered to undo her buttons, but she hadn't the strength to do so.

She was tired of feeling as she did; hungry for him, her needs only fulfilled in her deepest dreams. She wanted Derek, and he had just made it clear that he wanted her.

Perhaps it was time to make herself clearer. As honorable as Derek was, she suspected he did not want to find himself leg-shackled merely because he desired her. Rosalyn was not so naive that she didn't understand that a great fuss could be made about the four little letters before her name.

Lady.

She was Lady Rosalyn. Not the village milkmaid, not the vicar's daughter, but the daughter of an earl. Dalliances of the kind she had almost experienced with Derek generally ended with a ring on a girl's finger. But she didn't want marriage, and she suspected that Derek was not ready for it, either.

Rosalyn stood up and paced the room, contemplating her options. She should tell Derek that she would leave in the morning. His offer meant she needn't steal away from the house in the middle of the night, which—if she were honest with herself—had not seemed particularly appealing.

The path suddenly seemed so obvious: she would become Derek's mistress! Why deny herself? Her future was murky at best, and if Calder succeeded in his plans, she didn't have to worry about a future. What good would her virtue do her if she were dead?

And if Derek prevailed and Calder scampered away with his tail between his legs, then she would have the memory of her time with Derek to take with her.

Yes, it was all very clear. For the first time in a long while, no doubts troubled her.

Rosalyn rang for the maid. When the girl appeared, Rosalyn said, "Could you tell Lord Manchester that I must speak to him?"

"Shall I tell him that ye'll join him in the study, miss?"

Thinking it best not to get tongues wagging, especially if Derek preferred to keep their liaison a secret, Rosalyn replied, "Is there a courtyard? It is such a beautiful night, I believe I would like a stroll."

"Aye, miss. Ye go straight out the French doors." She pointed toward the far wall and Rosalyn noted the doors framed by lovely burgundy damask drapes and sheer ivory curtains.

Walking over to them, Rosalyn pushed back the curtain and looked out. The sky was pure black, with only the gleam of a full moon to cut through the darkness. It shone down on a cobblestone pathway that wound around thick hedges and scattered rosebushes until disappearing from sight behind the edge of a hawthorn tree.

It was perfect.

Glancing over her shoulder, Rosalyn said to the maid, "Please tell his lordship to meet me in the courtyard in a half hour. Then if you would be so kind to return to help me dress."

"Aye, miss." The girl bobbed and departed.

Rosalyn turned back and looked out into the midnight sky, a slow heat beginning to unfurl inside her. With a smile, she hastened to her trunks and got to work.

Nine

Derek stood in front of the fireplace in his bedroom, the blackened bricks and the faint smell of soot all that remained of past fires.

He glanced at his reflection in the mirror above the mantel. "You're a bloody bugger, old man. Can't even keep control around an innocent female." He shook his head. "Damn disgrace. Might as well call in your markers and tell the lads you're leaving the club."

The Pleasure Seekers never dallied with "ladies" and innocents, which made adhering to that rule fairly easy since each seemed generally exclusive to the other.

But not this time. Not with Rosalyn. She was both a lady and an innocent, as well as thoroughly enchanting and completely unpretentious.

The fact that her beauty did not affect her character made her that much more desirable. It made a man look beyond the outward appearance to what existed beneath, which was what Derek found so damn hard to resist.

He had met and bedded many beautiful women, but he had not yet come across one with a beautiful soul. Lady Rosalyn Carmichael left him at odds with himself.

A knock sounded on his door.

"Come," he barked.

"Y'r lordship?" a meek voice called from the doorway, bringing Derek's gaze over his shoulder to find one of the housemaids standing there.

She stared at him as though she thought flames would spew from his mouth. Margery, he believed was her name, one of the blacksmith's six daughters.

"Yes?" he said, tempering his tone. "What is it?"

She swallowed. "I have a message from the lady."

Derek's body tensed. He hadn't expected an answer so soon, and he suspected he knew what it was. He had undoubtedly frightened Rosalyn with his passion. He couldn't blame her for wanting to leave.

"What is the message?"

"The miss asked if ye would meet her in the courtyard in half an hour."

Derek frowned. The courtyard? Why would she want to meet there? And why hadn't she taken the convenient way out of her predicament and simply relayed her decision to depart through a disinterested party? He knew she had integrity and a surprising amount of grit, but he'd assumed she'd avoid facing him directly.

"My lord?" the maid prompted as he stood there mute.

"Fine," he said. "The courtyard it is."

Derek stared at the closed door for long minutes. He had promised Rosalyn that she would be safe from his advances, and yet the first opportunity he got, he had taken advantage.

It did no good to think about the fact that she hadn't struggled, or to recall how sweet and pliant her body had been against his, or how she had responded as though she had been waiting for the kiss, and only wished to scold him for taking so long to get about it. Christ, what was the use in wondering?

Grabbing his jacket from the chair, Derek shrugged into it. He glanced at the mantel clock. Only ten minutes had passed, but he couldn't wait another second in his room. He felt caged and edgy. Perhaps she wouldn't go, she'd give him another chance to prove himself.

They could play chess and discuss the philosophies of life. He could teach her about the configuration of the stars and planets, and their impact on the universe, and she could tell him stories about her life in Cornwall. They could be . . . companions.

Derek grimaced. Nevertheless, he could do it. He prided himself on his ability to follow through on whatever he set his mind to. Should Rosalyn decide to stay, he would apply himself to the task.

But as he stepped out into the heavily enshrouded night that quickly cloaked him in shadows, Derek couldn't help but wonder how he would get through even five minutes with Rosalyn without wanting to kiss her.

Jesus, he was in trouble.

•   •   •

Rosalyn had checked her appearance in the full-length mirror three times. She had changed even more times. Having never offered herself up as a mistress, she hadn't a clue what one might wear to prompt a seduction.

She finally settled on a dress that Lady Dane had bought for her during a shopping outing, insisting that Rosalyn have it. Rosalyn had been captivated by its beauty. The amount of bosom it showed seemed scandalous, which made it absolutely perfect. It was just what a soon-to-be-fallen woman would garb herself in.

"It grows late, m'lady," the young maid gently prompted. "His lordship will be waitin' for ye."

"Yes, thank you, Margery."

Rosalyn glanced at her reflection one final time. Her heart seemed to miss every third beat and her stomach was tied in a hundred knots. But she would not back down from her course of action now.

Summoning up a confident smile, Rosalyn turned to the young maid. "Wish me luck, Margery."

Margery smiled bashfully in return. "Good luck, miss. I hope ye get whatever y're lookin' for. I'm sure his lordship is goin' tae be speechless seein' ye dressed as ye are."

"You don't think it's too much?" Rosalyn asked.

"No, miss. Ye look regal."

A wave of calm rolled over Rosalyn. "Thank you, Margery. I don't know what I would have done without you."

She turned toward the French doors, the skirt of her dress belling around her as she hastened out into the cool night air.

The temperature had dipped since she arrived and the breeze nipped at her skin. She should have brought her shawl along. What good would her proposition do if she contracted the ague?

Her mind whirled as she followed the path leading to her rendezvous. Would he reject her offer out of hand? Or accept quickly?

Head up, Rosalyn continued on, lulled by the sound of crickets and the gentle tapping of her heeled slippers against the cobblestone walkway.

She didn't see Derek as she entered the courtyard, as he was partially hidden under a tall pine tree, but Derek saw her and he was awestruck by her transformation.

The woman standing in a pool of moonlight

with her golden blond hair in a luscious, loose wave down her back and her creamy shoulders sprinkled with stardust could not be the innocent young lady he had found himself increasingly fascinated with during the weeks since he had first met her.

This woman was self-assured and tantalizing, a female who could easily command any man's attention. Had they been standing in a ballroom, every male would be lined up for a dance and a chance to win her affections.

He knew in that moment that he couldn't keep away, either. Rosalyn glimmered like the brightest light in the sky, and all he wanted was to get close to her.

He quietly moved in behind her, hearing her soft sigh carried on the cool evening wind. He shrugged out of his jacket when he saw her shiver.

"Cold?" he murmured in her ear.

She swung around with a gasp, a hand to her chest. "You scared me."

"I apologize. I should have announced my presence, but I didn't want to break the spell. I was rendered speechless by you."

She stared at him with luminous blue eyes.

He looked down into those deep pools for a long moment before his gaze slid over her. "You are beautiful." The word was woefully inadequate—she was radiant, the most dazzling star in the sky.

A blush heated her cheeks. "You mean the dress."

"The dress is . . . stunning." He couldn't help studying her again, noticing the lush fullness of her breasts, the nipped-in waist, the way the material skimmed over her slim thighs. "But it's the woman wearing the dress that takes my breath away."

Her smile was brilliant. "Thank you."

"I hope you'll forgive me if I inquire as to the occasion."

They had arrived at the heart of the matter sooner than Rosalyn had expected, and she took a deep breath. "It seemed a night for dressing up."

"I'm honored, and I'll confess that I'm glad I'm the only one who gets to see you looking this way." He paused. "Dare I hope that you've forgiven my behavior earlier?"

"It's forgotten."

"But not forgiven? I don't blame you, and I'll

understand if you want to leave. I hope you will at least accept my apology."

"There's no apology necessary. I . . ." Rosalyn took another breath, trying to calm her racing nerves. "I wanted the kiss as much as you."

"Yes?"

"Surely you can tell that I'm . . . that I feel . . ."

Derek cupped her chin. "What do you feel?"

Rosalyn lifted her gaze to his, and found him as dark and mysterious as the midnight sky framing him. "I feel weak and strong, all at the same time. I feel incredibly bold and terribly frightened. I've never felt this way before."

"I feel it, too. I told myself to leave you alone. I thought I could. But then you walked into the courtyard, and I realized that all my hopes were in vain. I can't stay away from you."

"What should we do about it?"

"There's nothing we can do. You're here under my protection."

Rosalyn slid her hands up his chest, his white linen shirt cool beneath her fingertips. "Perhaps I don't want to be protected," she said softly against his lips. "At least not from you."

"Rosalyn," he said, an ache in his voice as he

wrapped his fingers lightly around her wrists to remove her hands, which nearly made Rosalyn falter.

"Hear me out. Please."

He stilled, except for his thumbs, which lightly caressed her skin, belying his desire to end what was brewing between them.

She leaned closer, her breasts lightly grazing his chest, which brought his gaze down to the soft mounds.

The dress had amazing boosting powers, giving her incredible fullness. Her flesh quivered with each breath she took. When Derek's gaze returned to her face, there was an intensity in his eyes that took her breath away.

"I've done a lot of thinking," she said, slowly sliding her hands down to the V of his shirt, where a tantalizing patch of bronze skin warmed her fingertips.

"And what have you been thinking about?"

"Us," she said, lifting the unbuttoned edge of his shirt and glimpsing the hard flesh of his chest.

"What about us?" he asked, a husky rasp to his words.

"Well . . . we've both confessed that there is an

attraction. And I thought that perhaps"—she rose up on tiptoe and boldly grazed his jaw with her lips—"you'd like to explore that attraction with me."

He took hold of her shoulders and stepped away from her. "Are you saying what I think you're saying?"

"What do you think I'm saying?"

"Jesus, Rosalyn, don't play games with me."

"I guess I'm not very good at this. I don't have a great deal of practice seducing men—this is my first time."

"Well, you did a damn fine job for your first time." He shook his head in confusion. "You're seducing me? This is priceless. I don't know whether to turn you over my knee, or—"

"Or what?"

"Never mind. What possessed you to—"

"Proposition you?"

"Yes. And it better not have anything to do with the reason you wore this dress."

"Why?"

"Because this isn't you. You're sweet and gentle—and innocent," he said, emphasizing the last word.

If he only knew. "Perhaps I don't wish to be any of those things anymore."

"It has nothing to do with not wanting to be that way. You *are* that way, and many men would kill for those qualities. Not every woman possesses them."

"I may be innocent in body and spirit, my lord, but I'm not as naive as you seem to think."

"I don't think you're naive. Just unschooled in the ways of men."

"That's why I want—"

"Don't say it."

Rosalyn huffed. "I don't understand you. You want me, yet you continue to keep me at a distance. Why?"

"Because one of us has to be rational about this, and clearly that is going to have to be me."

Feeling foolish and hurt, Rosalyn yanked her arm from his grasp, wanting nothing more than to vanish from sight and burn the horrible dress. What madness had come over her, to think that she could pull this off?

He took hold of her shoulders. "Where are you going?"

"Away from you. I don't know what I could have

been thinking, to want anything to do with you." She tried to move around him, but he easily blocked her path.

"Rosalyn, sweetheart—"

"Don't call me sweetheart," she fumed. "You've made yourself perfectly clear, my lord. I'm a nuisance and a bother and obviously not one of your oh-so-worldly women. I won't trouble you again. I'll have my things packed tonight and be ready to leave come the morning. Good night."

She tried to brush past him, but he halted her yet again. "Rosalyn, let's talk."

"There's nothing to talk about."

A disarming half-grin curled the corner of his mouth. "I'll have to disagree with you. A beautiful woman just offered me a precious gift that I don't deserve. I'm honored and humbled. But she doesn't understand that she deserves much more than a tumbling."

"Is that how you look at making love to me? A tumbling? Then perhaps you're right: I *do* deserve better. Now if you'll excuse me—"

Before she could move, Rosalyn found herself lifted from the ground and her body swung up into Derek's arms. "I'm not finished with you, and if I have to tie you down to make you listen, then I will."

"Put me down!"

He strode over to a wrought-iron bench and sat down, holding her close against his chest.

"Settle down," he said as she squirmed in his lap, hating how her traitorous body wanted him. "The sooner you hear what I have to say, the sooner you can slap me and storm into the house."

Rosalyn stared at him, aghast. "I would never slap you."

"Thank you. Now, let's discuss this proposition of yours."

She folded her arms across her chest and refused to look at him. "I thought you didn't want to refer to it as a proposition."

"I'm rethinking my position on that subject. Come on," he cajoled. "You can't blame me for being surprised."

"Shocked is more like it."

"All right. Shocked. You know, this is a first for me, too. You caught me off guard, which rarely happens to me."

Rosalyn couldn't understand why she felt so intractable. Her emotions seemed to be all over the place. She couldn't stop thinking about how she kept throwing herself at him and he kept throwing her back. There were many men who found her attractive, who had worked diligently to win her over. But she had never found any man to her taste, until Derek. From the moment he first smiled at her and she looked into his beautiful eyes, she had known.

Tears suddenly welled in her eyes. "Please, just let me go back to my room. I don't wish to discuss this. I've made a fool of myself, and I'd prefer not to drag out my humiliation any longer."

"You've done nothing to be ashamed of, Rosalyn. In fact, you were the brave one. You said things I wanted to say, but couldn't. All these weeks I've watched other men talk to you, dance with you, and touch you, and I've wanted to snap their necks. I didn't want anyone else to do with you what I wanted to do."

Rosalyn blinked up at him. "I never saw any of this."

"Because I had to contain it, which was damn hard. But I didn't go to those functions to seduce you; I was there to protect you. I couldn't lose sight of that."

"And now?"

"I still want to protect you, if you'll let me. I don't want anything to happen to you."

The reminder that Calder was still on the loose threw cold water onto the discussion.

"What if I don't want anything to happen to you?" she asked. "What am I supposed to do?"

"If Westcott somehow succeeds in finding us before I find him, then he would be detected before he stepped foot in the bailey." Derek tucked her closer, nestling her head beneath his chin. "You're safe here, love. Stay with me."

Rosalyn plucked at a button on his shirt. "But what about . . . you know."

A low chuckle rumbled in his chest. "That does pose a dilemma."

"It doesn't have to. It's not as though I'm expecting marriage."

"Why not?" He sounded surprised.

Rosalyn shrugged. "It's not for me."

"I thought every young lady dreamed of the day she would marry."

"Just as some men aren't suited to marriage, some women are not, either."

"That's an interesting way to put it. But I find it

even more interesting that you didn't say you didn't *want* to get married."

"But I did."

"No, you said you didn't expect it, and that it didn't suit you."

"Same thing."

"Not at all. But we'll come back to that later. I'd like to know what prompted you to approach me about this." Derek cupped her cheek. "You don't have any silly notion that you owe me something, do you?"

Rosalyn stiffened. "Absolutely not. I did what I did because it was what I felt at the time."

"So you don't feel that way anymore?"

If she were smart, she would say no, but she had never been a good liar. "I don't know how I feel. I think you want me, but then you don't."

"Rosalyn, I can't imagine a time when I won't want you. You tempt me at every turn, but—"

"Is there someone else? Is that the reason you keep rejecting me?"

"Jesus, I'm not rejecting you—and no, there's no one else."

She glanced up at the sky, wishing she was back in Cornwall, safe in her own bed, her mother and stepfather down the hall, and her stepbrother not planning her demise.

"Please," she said quietly, "let me up."

Reluctantly, he did as she asked. "Rosalyn," he began.

"Please don't say anything else—this is hard enough as it is. I don't know what I was thinking. I'm not some worldly woman who seduces men regularly. I'm just a girl from a small hamlet in Cornwall."

"And that's the very reason I'm so drawn to you. You're unaffected and genuine. I wouldn't have given your offer a second thought if you were as jaded and cynical as I am."

Rosalyn turned to face him. "You're not jaded and cynical."

"You don't know me as well as you think. I've done some things I'm not proud of."

"We all have. We wouldn't be human otherwise."

"I don't want to spoil you. I couldn't live with myself if I did. You say you don't want marriage, but what if you should change your mind? What if you regret making love to me?"

Rosalyn laid her palm against his cheek, as he

had done to her minutes earlier. "That won't happen. I've hardly thought of anything else since I met you," she confessed.

"What if I grow attached to you? What if *I* think of marriage? What then?"

His remark took her by surprise. "I . . ." Rosalyn shook her head. "I don't know."

"Did the thought ever cross your mind?"

"No," she said honestly. "Is that why you're so hesitant? Because you think I'll expect you to marry me? I won't. But neither do I want to die a virginal spinster."

Derek took a length of her hair in his hand. "You're far from a spinster, and a long way off from your final reward."

"At three and twenty, I am what most people would consider on the shelf. As for what tomorrow holds . . ." She sighed and thought of Calder. "I just don't want to spend the rest of my life regretting what I *didn't* do. Can you understand that?"

"More than you know."

She stepped away and walked over to smell a budding rose. "I'm sorry if I put you in an awkward position, and I'll understand if you feel uncomfortable with me now. This won't happen again, so you needn't worry I'll be cornering you in every deserted courtyard."

"I'm not worried. But I would be gravely disappointed if you chose not to corner me again. If that were the case, I would be compelled to corner you." He closed the distance between them and plucked the rose she had just been smelling, then traced it softly over her lips.

"If you still want me, I'll come to you at midnight. If you don't open the door, I'll understand. This is your decision, Rosalyn. I would never want you to do something you'd regret. Neither of us could live with that."

Placing the rose in the palm of her hand, he turned and walked away. Rosalyn watched him disappear down the darkened path, and with her heart beating wildly, she wondered what she had just gotten herself into.

Ten

$\mathcal{D}$erek glanced at the clock on the mantel: quarter to midnight. Soon he'd be knocking on Rosalyn's door. Soon they'd have this matter settled. He hoped to hell that she barred the door with iron rods—about as much as he prayed she'd take him into her arms and into her bed.

It was insanity. What were they doing? What was *he* doing? He felt as nervous as a green lad. He had well earned his membership in the Pleasure Seekers, and it was a point of honor to give his women as much pleasure as they gave him.

But this was Rosalyn. She was an entirely different

type of woman; bedding her meant too much to feel casual about it.

He raked a hand through his hair. He should have called the whole thing off instead of calling her bluff. All night he had expected her to send a note round telling him that she had not been thinking clearly, but no such luck. The house had been eerily subdued. If he didn't know better, he might think everyone knew where he would be when the clock struck twelve, adding another layer to his anxiety.

As the minutes ticked down, Derek headed out of his bedroom toward Rosalyn's.

For half a minute he actually told himself that if Rosalyn really wanted him, then there was nothing wrong. They were two consenting adults; no one was forcing them to do anything they weren't perfectly willing to do.

So why did he feel like some lecherous swine salivating over a lost lamb?

And why didn't he turn on his heel and go back to his room, lock the door, and console himself with a finely aged bottle of brandy? Just because he had said he would come for her at midnight did not actually mean he had to go. He had choices. Options.

But none of that had him heading back to his room.

He passed through the vestibule that separated the east wing from the west. So much for his theory of putting them on opposite ends of the house. So much for his touted willpower. He had held out for all of five minutes after her incredible offer, his protests halfhearted.

As he rounded the corner, his musings were cut short as something heavy cracked into the back of his head, sending him sprawling to the ground, out cold.

Rosalyn twisted the tie on her wrapper around her finger over and over again, consumed with the clock.

Derek would be knocking on her door in less than two minutes. A few minutes after that, she could very well be a fallen woman.

When the knock came, Rosalyn jumped. The moment had arrived. Swallowing down her nerves, she yanked the ties of her wrapper so tightly she could barely breathe.

Then she went to the door, inhaled a deep breath, and opened it. But the person standing on the other side was not Derek.

"Did I wake you?"

Rosalyn blinked. "What are you doing here?"

She didn't know why Ethan was at her bedroom door at midnight, but she could just imagine what Derek would do if he found his half-brother there. She had to get rid of Ethan before he arrived.

"I saw your light on and wanted to see how you fared on your first day at Castle Gray," he said. "No ghosts to haunt you, I hope? Although we do have a few skeletons in our closet."

"You do realize the time."

"Time is relative," he said with a shrug. "May I come in?"

"No, that would be improper."

He gave her a wicked smile. "I've never been very proper."

"I can see that."

He stepped past her. "Derek gave you his mother's old room. How quaint." He turned to her. "Lady Emmaline liked to stay as far away from her husband as possible. I must say that I'm surprised Derek would want you at such a distance. Had it been me, I would have put you in the suite next to mine and promptly oiled the hinges on the adjoining door."

Rosalyn closed her fingers around the top of her wrapper and hugged the material to her chest.

Ethan laughed. "Have no fears, sweet. I don't intend to ravage you—unless you'd like me to. I aim to please."

"My lord," Rosalyn began.

"I'm not a lord. Just a lowly bastard living off his brother's largesse. Not that I mind, of course. I consider what belongs to Derek as being rightfully mine. I was firstborn, after all. In simple terms: I'm owed. But enough of that," he said, waving a dismissive hand. "I feel like celebrating."

"And the occasion?"

"Need there be one?"

"This isn't—"

"If I remember correctly, there is a nice bottle of port in the cabinet of that side table." He strode across the room and reached inside the cabinet, blowing off the dust that had settled on the bottle before lifting it into the light, where red prisms glittered. "Magnificent." He pried out the glass stopper and held the bottle to his lips, hesitating only long enough to offer her the first swig.

"No, thank you."

"Suit yourself." He took a mouthful, sighing loudly after he swallowed. Glancing sideways at her, he said, "Not very sophisticated, was it? But Derek likes to keep the liquor under lock and key. God forbid anyone should get jocular in this mausoleum, least of all me.

"I tend to keep my own supply, but my sibling also enjoys his petty vindictiveness by having the storekeepers refuse to sell to me. Since the entire village is under his thumb, most will not deny him. But," he finished with a grin, "I'm not without resources."

"Is all this animosity between the two of you truly necessary?" Rosalyn asked.

"I can't imagine a day without it."

"But doesn't it grow old?"

Ethan shrugged. "I'll confess that the lad has learned to curb his temper much better than when he was a do-gooding adolescent."

"I presume you rebel against doing good?"

He gestured with the bottle. "You are catching on, sweet. I knew you would."

"Don't you think it's time to end this feud? Your father is dead, and you are both adults."

Ethan regarded her as though she had sprouted horns and a forked tail. "Perish the thought. I feel it's my purpose in this world to annoy my self-righteous sibling. Certainly you wouldn't want to deny me the pleasure?"

A voice suddenly interjected, "Is that why you hit me on the back of the head like the coward you are?"

Rosalyn whirled around to find Derek in the doorway, a line of blood trickling from his temple.

She rushed to him and took his face between her hands. "My God, what happened?"

Derek glanced over at Ethan, fury in his eyes. "Why don't you ask my brother?"

Ethan perched on the corner of Rosalyn's bed, the bottle of port nestled in front of him. "Certainly you're not implying that I had anything to do with your injury? You were always clumsy. I recall countless times when you tripped over your own two feet. And here you are as laird. It defies probability. I had thought you'd have tumbled off a cliff by now."

"I'm sure that's exactly what you'd have liked. Perhaps you would have even hastened along my untimely departure with a hand to my back."

"I'm nothing if not accommodating," Ethan replied lightly.

"You bloody bastard," Derek spat through gritted teeth, forcing Rosalyn to move in front of him as he stepped toward his brother.

"Enough," she said softly but insistently. "Please get on the bed."

"It seems your convenient spill has earned you an invitation to the lady's bed," Ethan taunted. "Count yourself a lucky man."

Rosalyn's grip tightened on Derek's arm when he tensed, and she glared at Ethan. "I must see to your brother's wounds. Could you please get some clean towels?" She had towels; she just wanted Ethan to leave. His look said he recognized her ploy.

"Anything for you, my love," he replied, rising with a flourish.

"If I see you near this room again," Derek said in a barely controlled tone, "you'll be a eunuch before your next breath."

"More empty threats. Nevertheless, I'll leave. Watching you bleed grows boring, and the night is still young. Do feel better, brother." Ethan raised the bottle in a taunting salute, then turned to go.

At the door, he nearly ran into Darius. "Ah, the cavalry has arrived. The wounded lie yonder." Whistling, he disappeared into the corridor.

"Good Lord, lad, what's happened tae ye?" his uncle exclaimed.

"It would appear I've been injured," Derek muttered as Rosalyn poured water from a carafe on her bedside table into a bowl.

Rosalyn grabbed one of her monogrammed hankies and dipped it in the cool water.

"Here, let me clean you up."

Derek reached for the wet handkerchief. "I can do it," he said gruffly.

Rosalyn held the cloth away from him. "I'm not going to argue with you. Now lie there and remain still, otherwise this may hurt more than I intend."

Darius hooted. "Listen to the lass, boy. She's not one tae abide your foul temper. Best do as you're told."

Derek scowled at his uncle. "Is there something you need? Or are you just here to watch me bleed to death?"

Rosalyn snorted. "What melodrama."

"Pardon me?" Derek said as he shifted his gaze to her.

Rosalyn met his glare without flinching. "I said, you're being overly dramatic. You won't bleed to death, but you will have an unsightly lump and a prodigious headache in the morning."

"And how do you know I'm not injured elsewhere? Have you checked?"

"No, I haven't. Are you injured elsewhere? Or is this simply a ploy for attention? I've seen two-year-olds do a better job of it than you."

Derek caught Darius's muffled laugh, but he was too preoccupied with his nurse to care. "Oh? And how many two-year-olds have you attended, may I ask?"

"The hills and valleys of Cornwall were filled with young ones playing and ultimately taking spills. And they sounded remarkably like you do now. So if you'd be so kind as to remain quiet, I would be grateful."

"She told you, lad," Darius hooted. "Aye, she certainly did."

"You have until the count of three to remove yourself from this room," Derek warned his uncle, his bloody head throbbing as if someone had used it for a drum.

When he got his hands on Ethan, he would

wring the rotter's neck. Derek had little doubt it was his half-brother's welcome-home gesture, one that could have been fatal had the blow been harder.

He'd had enough of feeling some twisted obligation to the man. He should have thrown Ethan out years ago. No one would blame him; everyone in the clan knew Ethan was a troublemaker. More than just Derek had fallen victim to him.

Derek had been pulling Ethan out of one scrape after the next for years—why, he didn't know. Once he might have thought it would be nice to have a brother, but he damn well didn't have to tolerate it anymore.

Especially if it involved Rosalyn in any way. Derek had caught glimpses of something he didn't like in Ethan's eyes. Something that looked a great deal like infatuation.

"Happy now?"

Rosalyn's voice brought Derek back to the moment. He glanced up to find her staring down at him, hands on her hips. "What?"

"I asked if you were happy, now that you've chased away your uncle."

Derek snorted. "If Darius left, it was because

he wanted to. Not even the earth splintering beneath his feet could get that man to move if he didn't feel like it. So please retract your claws—I've had enough violence for one day." Wincing, Derek sat up.

"Goodness," Rosalyn huffed, pushing him back as she adjusted the pillows. "You are obstinate."

Her long hair brushed his cheek. Both its feel and its smell tantalized him, reminding him forcefully of why he had traversed the castle's darkened corridors in the first place.

Her wrapper had loosened, exposing a creamy section of bosom, and her nipples were lightly peaked and pressing against her thin nightgown.

"I'm sorry I ruined our evening," he said.

A soft blush stained her cheeks when she noticed the proximity of her breasts to his face, and she took a step back. The realization seemed to sink in on both of them at the same time that he was not only in her bedroom, but in her bed.

"Nothing has to happen, you know," he told her. "I really didn't expect that it would. I'm happy just to spend time with you."

"I haven't changed my mind."

"You haven't?"

"No. I won't lie and say I'm not nervous. But I want this. I want you."

Derek tugged her toward him, seating her beside him on the bed. "I want you, too."

Had she glanced down at his trousers, she would have seen the evidence of that desire. He was rock-hard and in desperate need of a plunge into the ice-cold depths of the loch, which was where he figured he'd be heading as soon as she realized she didn't want to waste her gift on him.

But she rose to her feet, her gaze never leaving his as she undid the tie on her robe and let the silky material slip to her feet, framing her like a nymph rising from the sea. Her nightgown outlined the lush curves of her body: the fullness of breasts that sloped upward, the slender waist and small hips, the toes peeping out from beneath the hem.

Her hands trembled as she eased first one strap off her shoulder, then the other. The silk caressed her as it slid slowly down her body, halting briefly at her nipples to taunt him before it slithered the rest of the way, leaving her gloriously naked.

Eleven

*R*osalyn stood utterly still, feeling as though she was affixed to the floor like a breathing statue. This was full exposure in front of a man. And not just any man, but the one she would give her innocence to.

"You're pale as a ghost," Derek said, concern in his tone as he pulled Rosalyn down into his arms. "I told you, love, you don't have to do this."

"No," she said, shaking her head. "It's not that."

"Then what?"

She reached out and lightly touched his wound. "Do you think that Calder may have found us?"

Derek wrapped his arms around her shoulders and hugged her close. "Is that what's bothering you?

You think your stepbrother has found out where you are?"

Rosalyn had not been concerned for herself. "He could have been the one who hurt you."

"Trust me, love, Calder is not within a hundred miles of here. I'd know."

"But—"

Derek silenced her with a finger to her lips. "He's not in Castle Gray. He'd not only have to be invisible, but a damn fine magician." He turned her face up to his. "Don't worry."

Derek could see she still had her doubts, and he felt a renewed determination to protect her, no matter what it took. The thought of anyone hurting her was unbearable.

Nothing had ever scared him before. He had looked death in the face more than once and come out unscathed.

But this was not his life, it was Rosalyn's. She was coming to mean a great deal to him. Each day she filled more and more of the empty space in his heart.

Long ago, he had reconciled himself to the fact that there was no such thing as a soul mate. Men and women could be companions and lovers, but there didn't seem to be more to it than that.

Love was a fairy tale that would never find him, and he had accepted that. It had long been an unspoken understanding that he would someday marry Megan Trelawny. She was young and beautiful and immune to the hardships of living in the Highlands, as she had been born and bred to the land.

His clan and the Trelawnys had once been mortal enemies, but that was decades past. The rift had healed, though memories remained. It had seemed sensible to merge the two clans, uniting strong bands of Highlanders. The Trelawnys' property bordered Castle Gray's. Marriage would make them allies.

But deep down, Derek knew that what truly divided him from Rosalyn was her English heritage. Outsiders had tried and failed in his country. His mother had ended up miserable and bitter, longing for country parties and grand balls, beautiful gowns and proper gentlemen.

Eventually Rosalyn would miss that as well. Castle Gray was isolated, a world unto itself, and while he reveled in keeping the outside world at bay, Rosalyn would long for something more. Something he couldn't give her, as his father hadn't been able to give his mother.

Still, knowing all that, Derek did what he had wanted to do all day. He pulled her close and kissed her, softly at first, savoring her sweet mouth and the allure of her response.

The kiss quickly turned heated as she twined her arms around his neck and pulled him tighter, her breasts a warm, soft weight against his chest.

He cupped one firm globe and heard her swift intake of breath as his thumb swept over her nipple, grazing the taut peak.

"You're so beautiful," Derek murmured, brushing his mouth lightly over hers before skimming down her throat, feeling her heart fluttering like a hummingbird.

He grazed her collarbone, her breathing becoming rapid with excitement. He wanted to go slow with her, let her get used to his touch. He savored each piece of her silky skin, his body taut and explosive. He wanted her so badly, every part of him ached.

Derek eased down to the lush valley between her breasts, slowly running his tongue over the full swells, aching to taste her nipples.

He reveled in her moan as he drew her nipple into his mouth and gently sucked. She tossed her head back and clasped the back of his head.

He licked a path to the other rigid nub and flicked it with the tip of his tongue, going a bit faster with each pass until Rosalyn was writhing in his arms.

He lowered her to her back as he eased partially on top of her, his mouth and hands massaging her nipples until they were two distended points, swollen from his touch.

He slid his hand down her stomach, feathering his fingertips over the smooth, flat surface, feeling her shiver as he found a sensitive spot.

Derek took his time working inexorably toward the downy curls and the sweet pearl within. Her legs were clenched tight, but he slipped his hand between her thighs and kneaded the tense muscles until she became pliant, opening up for him.

"I won't hurt you," he murmured against her temple. "I would never hurt you."

Rosalyn turned, and for the first time since Derek had initiated their lovemaking, she kissed him, her mouth sweet over his, her hand dipping inside the open front of his shirt to stroke his chest.

A primitive growl rumbled up inside him, and

he pressed his lips tighter to hers, wanting to devour her, his control at the breaking point.

When he parted her nether lips, his fingers sliding into her wet heat, he knew she was almost ready for him. She arched up against his hand as he began to tease her sensitive nub, her whimper an erotic sound in his ear.

Her eyes were closed and he kissed the lids, waiting for her gaze to focus on him. Her eyes looked dewy in the muted light, but the desire in their depths nearly did him in.

"Come," he quietly directed, changing his position to lean back against the headboard, moving Rosalyn between his open thighs. Her head tilted back against his chest, her hard nipples thrust upward, the new angle giving him the ability to see the entire landscape of her ripe body, and letting her watch what he was doing to her.

"Does this feel good?"

"Mmm," she purred, the sound driving him wild. "I want to touch you."

"You will, love. This is for you now. Feel how sensitive your nipples are."

As he hoped, his words excited her. Her moisture drenched his finger as he slid back and forth, his movements growing faster, riding just the tip of her hot point. Her hips slanted up and back; her breasts thrust into his hands.

She was beyond anything but the pleasure he was giving her, her soft pleas telling him that she was on the edge. When he gently squeezed her nipples, she cried out, tightening around the finger he eased into her, the rippling waves clenching him, making him hunger for her to clench a different part of his body.

When she sighed and closed her eyes, her body becoming liquid against his, Derek repositioned her, cradling her in the crook of his arm and resting her cheek against his shoulder.

Only the sound of their breathing filled the room as Derek lightly stroked her arm, a feeling of satisfaction and peace stealing over him. He didn't have to make love to her to enjoy a sense of completion.

He had thought Rosalyn had drifted off to sleep, but when he turned to look down at her, he found her gaze on his face, her hair twined around his hand. His fingers seemed to reach for it without conscious thought.

He stroked the tips along her jaw. "How do you feel?"

She sighed and stretched like a contented cat.

"Luscious," she murmured. "I never knew it could be that way. My dreams were no equal."

"You're a sensual woman. Any man would be lucky to call you his own."

"Am I yours, then?"

It was a question he couldn't answer. He had no right to believe Rosalyn was his. He'd had no right to even touch her, but he had become so consumed with her he thought he would go crazy.

Derek didn't know how he'd feel when the day came for her to leave. And she would go, that he knew. She longed for Cornwall, and his place was here—with Megan Trelawny.

"You don't belong to any man, love," he replied softly.

She tucked her chin, not allowing him to see how she had taken his remark. But it was better for both of them not to mistake desire for a lifetime, no matter how he felt about her.

She shifted then, surprising him by moving on top of his body. "Can I touch you now?"

"Be my guest."

At her first tentative touch, Derek fought the surge of his body. Her fingertip glided over the dent in his chin and the light stubble on his jaw before traveling down his neck, every muscle in his body becoming hot and taut.

"You're lovely," Rosalyn murmured as her hands moved over the buttons of his shirt, her heart racing with each bit of flesh she exposed until his chest lay bare before her. She traced the defined muscles, sweeping lightly over the satiny pebbles of his nipples.

She applied her tongue to one, kissing and then gently sucking. Air hissed between his teeth, and Rosalyn glanced up at him.

"I can barely feel you, but what I do feel is making me crazy."

His hands slid down her waist and around to cup her buttocks, kneading her flesh as he pressed her tighter against him.

Rosalyn could feel his arousal, and her body responded, her hips gyrating slowly, her gaze never leaving his as his eyes turned from a steely gray-blue to a smoky sapphire.

Rosalyn grew bolder, her fingers pressing into his flesh, her nails gently raking his skin. She applied her lips to every spot she could reach, taking her time in some areas and quickly sampling others.

Rock-hard muscle shifted beneath her fingertips as she inched her way up his body, kissing his neck as he had kissed hers, his body tensing when she ran the tip of her tongue along the outside of his ear. She would never have known how exquisitely sensitive that part of her body could be, had he not shown her.

She sat up and tugged at his shirt. "Please . . . take it off."

His powerful thighs flexed and his stomach muscles clenched as he rose up to shrug out of his shirt. Rosalyn tossed it to the floor and wrapped her hands around his upper arms. She had never seen arms so large, muscles so fully developed and firm. Everything about him was superb.

Leaning down, she kissed him. He gripped the back of her head to hold her there. Her nipples lightly grazed his chest, stirring that heady sensation he had evoked only a short while earlier.

She would never have imagined that something so powerful could take over her body, as though he thoroughly controlled her, and she would not have believed it could not happen again so soon. But as Derek took her breasts in the palms of his hands, a raging hunger awoke inside her. She ached for the pleasure he could give.

Derek rolled her to her back. She loved the heavy weight of him, how solid and real he felt. How secure she felt in his arms.

Instinctively, she opened her thighs when he moved on top of her. She knew what he could do, but she wanted to give him pleasure, too.

"What should I do?"

"Nothing," he said in a husky rasp against her ear as he kissed her neck.

"I want to make love to you."

"I don't want you to hate me in the morning."

Rosalyn laid her hand on his cheek. "I could never hate you." Neither could she imagine giving her innocence to any other man.

She reached for the top button on his trousers. When he grabbed hold of her hand, Rosalyn thought he would deny her. Instead, he looked her in the eyes and said, "If you want me to stop, I will. I won't do anything you don't want me to do. All right?"

"Yes."

"Good. Then close your eyes and let me show you new delights."

Instead of removing his trousers, he raised himself off her, as though he intended to get up from the bed, but then he turned to lie with his head between her thighs.

"What are you—*Ooh*," she moaned, her back arching off the bed as his tongue speared the very heart of her, flicking her swollen bud, laving it back and forth until Rosalyn thought she would die of pleasure.

Never could she have imagined anything like this. It seemed decadent and so very sinful, but she didn't want Derek to stop.

Her breath left her in a rush as he drew the pointed nub into his mouth, each tug sending lightning through her veins. When he pressed tighter against her and reached up to play with her nipples, the rippling convulsions broke over her again like a wave, leaving her body replete and her limbs feeling boneless.

Through drowsy lids, she watched Derek rise from the bed, his fingers deftly undoing the remaining buttons on his trousers until they fell free. Her focus sharpened on his jutting manhood, thick and long, and the taut sacs snug at the base.

Derek caught the look in her eyes. She had said she wouldn't regret what happened between them, but the heat of passion could make rationality take flight. His own included.

And looking at Rosalyn now, her nipples tight and rosy from his mouth, her arms reaching out to him in anticipation, and her eyes heavy with desire, Derek knew he couldn't resist her. It was that simple. And perhaps, deep down, he wanted to be the first man who made love to her.

Derek took her into his arms, silencing her questions with his mouth until she was soft and compliant.

Then he lowered himself to the bed with Rosalyn on top of him, her breasts a taunting pressure against his chest. He lifted her slightly, taking one nipple into his mouth while his fingers played with the other. She writhed, her hips instinctively moving against his.

He rocked upward, his shaft sliding along her silken folds, the head scoring the heated pearl nestled there, making contact with each pass. He was beginning to understand her sounds, the erotic noises she made, what excited her the most, and he strove to give it to her.

When he thought she was ready, he sat her up.

He swept tendrils of hair from her face and smiled at how beautifully rumpled she was.

"Now?" she said softly, passion in her lush blue eyes.

"In this position, you can take control. It's up to you how fast or slow we go. Just sit down on top of me."

She leaned forward, her hands curled around his shoulders. Her gaze moved from his face to his shaft as she eased down onto him.

She bit her lip and closed her eyes. "It feels so . . . full."

He knew there would be some pain the first time. "If you want to stop—"

"No," she answered swiftly, lifting up a bit and easing back down, getting used to him, adjusting to his size.

Never in his life had he bedded a virgin; he hadn't wanted the responsibility of being the first. He had always gravitated toward women who were as versed in the sexual act as he was.

Without warning, she sat down fully on him, her swift intake of breath the only sound she made. Her eyes were shut tight, and Derek knew she had felt the stab of pain from the breaking of her maidenhead.

When she opened her eyes, everything she felt was written there. Desire, surprise, an awakening to carnal pleasures. But not hate. Not disgust. None of the things he feared. She truly wanted him.

His shaft, hard and throbbing inside her, moved out of reflex.

Her eyes widened and she instinctively clenched her inner lips. She was deep and wet around him, and he fisted his hands in the sheets to keep from gripping her waist and showing her movements.

She leaned down and laved his nipple, whispering, "You taste so good."

That broke his control. He wrapped his hand around the back of her neck and pulled her down to him, kissing her fiercely as he thrust up inside her.

She groaned and matched his thrust, sliding down flush against him, taking him in as far as she could and then lifting up, her movements becoming faster and more frantic.

When she sat straight up, Derek cupped her breasts, flicking her nipples with his thumbs and watching her ride him. Her head was tossed back, her long silky hair skimming his thighs with each downward glide of her body, her slim legs gripping him, her hands settled behind her, giving her leverage to move.

Her sweet moans resonated through his blood. Only sheer will kept him from finding his own release; he wanted her to come with a man's rod inside her, to experience all the ways a woman could find pleasure.

Derek heard her breathing quicken, and her body began to tense. She was close. He rubbed his forefinger over the pink pearl so lushly displayed in her current position, and watched her go over the edge.

Her back stiffened as a wave of deep, clenching spasms gripped him like a fist, pumping at his flesh, taking him to the brink. He pulled out of her and found his release.

She collapsed against his chest, and he stroked her back until she fell asleep in his arms.

Twelve

Derek got little accomplished the next morning as he stared out his office window at Devil's Crag in the distance.

He had slipped out of Rosalyn's bed in the middle of the night after making love to her twice more—which was three more times than he should have. But she had bewitched him, made him insatiable for her.

He hadn't wanted to leave her side, but the household staff woke early. Regardless of Rosalyn's avowals that she wished to be a fallen woman, he didn't want her to suffer the consequences.

She had rolled toward the spot he had vacated, her arm flung out, his name a whisper on her lips, striking Derek like an arrow to his heart and embedding itself permanently there.

"Christ," he muttered, running a hand through his hair and grimacing as his fingers grazed the lump at the back of his head.

When Derek had been in London and a few potentially fatal events had befallen him, there had been no one who could have staged those accidents except Ethan. The strange occurrences hadn't begun until his brother had arrived in town.

A few times Derek had tried to befriend Ethan. He was the only brother Derek had, after all. After getting over the initial shock of his father's betrayal and how it had destroyed his mother, Derek had come to understand how Ethan might feel, recognizing the stigma of being labeled a bastard, never hearing the word *son*.

Derek doubted that Ethan had started out to make trouble. But once his half-brother had set himself on that course, there had been no diverting him from it, and all Derek's attempts to build a bridge had been met with resistance and often chaos.

They had pulverized each other so many times, Derek had lost count, with an even spread of wins and losses between them. Perhaps they were so evenly matched because they had been sired by the same father.

They had both been sent away to school, Derek by his father and Ethan by Derek's mother. Whatever would tweak her husband's nose, Lady Emmaline felt compelled to do.

They had attended different academies, but while Derek had focused on learning the things he hoped would make him a success in life, Ethan had made it a point to return with an even greater dedication to obtaining what he thought belonged to him, becoming a man so well polished he could fit in just about anywhere, his skills for disingenuous charm honed to a rapier's edge.

No matter how diligently Ethan strove to be accepted, though, the taint of his birth burned him like a brand.

"Still nursin' y'r wound, I see."

Derek turned from the window to find Darius sauntering in. "I'm still alive, if that was your concern." Derek strode to his desk, where he would likely continue to get nothing done.

His mind was preoccupied with thoughts of Rosalyn, consumed with images of their lovemaking—the sweet, tight heat between her wet nether lips, the taut nipples thrust heavenward, marked by his mouth and bobbing as he thrust inside her, her thighs hard around his flanks, his hands gripping her soft flesh, his body thrumming from her moans. He wondered how she would feel about him now, when there was no taking back what had happened between them.

"Y'r head is too hard tae crack," Darius chuckled as he headed straight for the sideboard to drag out the aged whisky, even though it was barely past the morning meal. "'Twould take much more tae send ye tae your maker—an anvil, perhaps, or the weight of a house."

"Your obvious distress about my welfare is touching. Is there anything I can do for you, or is it your intent to drink yourself into a stupor before midday?"

Darius eyed him over his shoulder, his bushy brows making a V in his forehead. "'Twould seem the knock on y'r skull did little tae improve y'r surly disposition."

"Having one's head nearly removed from one's shoulders puts one in a less than positive frame of mind."

"There's no need tae be gettin' snippy, lad. I'm still y'r elder, laird or not."

"And will you put me over your knee and tan my hide? I'm a bit too old for that."

Darius grunted. "Y'r father would turn over in his grave if he could hear the way ye speak tae me."

Having been treated to that refrain often over the years, Derek ignored it. He dropped down into the chair behind his desk and laced his hands across his stomach, regarding his uncle's back.

Darius had always been good at laying on the guilt. His beleaguered-old-man act was quite impressive at times and garnered sympathy from those who didn't know him as well as Derek did.

Darius was far more cagey than people suspected, and yet Derek had never given his uncle's malcontent a second thought—until recently.

He had meant to apologize to Darius after questioning his loyalty at the inn, but something had stopped him. He couldn't get the thought out of his head that Darius's grumbling was more than just the ramblings of an old man.

There had been a few times when Derek had suspected his uncle of planning the accidents that had befallen him; Darius had been around during several of the suspicious events.

Part of Derek continued to scoff at the idea that either his uncle or brother—or perhaps both together—were striving for his demise. Regardless of their foibles, Darius and Ethan were his kin.

And if Derek should succumb to one of his "accidents," Ethan and Darius would be the first suspects his clan looked at, as the two with the most to gain.

No, something else was going on. He was missing something right in front of him. But he'd be damned if he could figure out what it was.

"Are ye plannin' tae stare at the tips of y'r shoes all day, lad?" Darius asked, well into his second glass of whisky. "Or might ye be contemplatin' the betterment of the clan?" He gestured toward the east-facing window with his drink. "The natives have been restless since ye returned with the English lass. There's rumblin' about ye takin' up where y'r father left off, and that there'll be nothin' but discontent at Castle Gray if ye become involved with the lady."

Derek strove to remain impassive. What he did

was his bloody business; he would tolerate no one telling him how to live his life, or with whom.

Yet how could he keep Rosalyn from being touched by the scorn of his people? They already disliked her without even knowing her. Damn his parents and their endless feuding.

"Is there a question somewhere in that remark?" Derek queried, regarding his uncle with practiced disinterest.

Darius frowned and placed his glass on the sideboard. "I hate it when ye play obtuse. Ye know exactly what I'm sayin'. I'm tryin' tae warn ye of what may be comin'. For y'r own sake, ye should send the lass away."

"No."

Darius stared at him incredulously. "No? Just like that?"

"Just like that: Rosalyn stays. Anyone who doesn't like it can leave."

"These are y'r people, man, are ye forgettin' that?"

Derek held his uncle's gaze. "Are you questioning my loyalty?"

"Of course not," Darius blustered as he shuffled toward the empty fireplace, glancing at the spot above the mantel where a picture of Derek's mother had once resided—first revered and adored, later loathed and resented.

Many a night Derek had heard a glass breaking in his father's office. The next morning he would spy a maid cleaning up the shattered remains and see another tear in the portrait's delicate canvas, the spray of alcohol marring its beauty.

It was as though his father was trying to systematically blot out her very existence.

The sound of a commotion in the hallway propelled Derek out of his seat. He had barely taken a single step before a whirlwind in a calico dress pranced into his office, her pitch-black hair hanging wild down her back and her softly rounded cheeks pink from dashing across the fields from her brother's property to his.

"Ye rotten scalawag!" Megan Trelawny said with a cheeky grin. "Not a single word tae tell me ye were returnin'. Ye should be tied tae the post and given the strap."

"You would be the one wielding it, I suppose?" Derek rejoined with a laugh, barely making it around his desk before Megan flung herself into his arms and hugged him tight.

"It's so good tae have ye home," she murmured fervently against his chest. "Never leave."

Derek returned her hug. She had blossomed into a beautiful young woman, but to him she would always be the scamp who dashed about the countryside muddying herself and making mischief.

"Now," she said briskly as she untangled her arms from around his neck. "Who is this English lady ye've brought home with ye? I hear she's quite a beauty, with hair paler than a morning sun and skin like rare Chinese porcelain."

Megan's description was far better than Derek could have come up with on his own. "Perhaps you'd like to take a seat?" he suggested, gesturing to the chair in front of his desk.

She canted a brow at him and put her hands on her hips. "Take a seat, is it? My, how very proper we are." She marched over to the chair and plunked down into it. Instead of settling back, she reached down and pulled the hem of her gown up to mid-thigh to unstrap her dirk.

Glancing up, she caught him watching and said, "Ye'll be keepin' your eyes in your sockets if ye ken what's good for ye."

"I'm just wondering why you continue to carry that thing."

"Protection," she answered, checking the sharpness of the blade. "Wouldn't want someone comin' up on me unprepared. I've got tae get Kerry tae make a bigger holster for my thigh, though. The bleedin' thing keeps pokin' me. If ye haven't noticed, your high and mighty lordship, I've got a woman's figure now." She treated him to an impish pose.

"I've noticed."

She harrumphed. "Not that ye've done anything about it."

"What would you like me to do?"

"If I have tae tell ye, then I think ye'll be needin' tae talk with Kerry."

Kerry, her oldest brother, had been laird of Clan Trelawny since his father had handed over the mantle of control three years ago.

Kerry was the last person Derek wanted to speak to about anything, especially his sister, whom he clearly adored, as did her seven other brothers. Megan, as the only girl, was doted upon.

None of her brothers had been overly happy when her father had announced that she would marry Derek when she was old enough.

Derek had said neither yes or no, simply accepting that Megan would someday be his wife. But somewhere along the way, complications had arisen. One amazing complication named Rosalyn Carmichael.

"Ye're not really worried about Kerry, are ye?"

Derek realized he hadn't heard a word Megan had said to him. "Worried about Kerry?" he scoffed, reaching over to pinch her cheek, much as he did when she was a child. "Not in the least. I still remember when he was a squat little toad, sinking in the mud at the watering hole because he was so chubby."

"Ye are a wicked man tae be bringin' up such a thing." Megan giggled. "Poor Kerry! He was up tae his knees in that muck when me brothers managed tae heave him from it. Tae this day, we are forbidden tae mention it, and he turns the most unflattering shade of red if we do. He wouldn't appreciate your reference tae his waistline, either. He likes tae believe he's big-boned. So shame on you." She wagged her finger at him, but amusement reflected in her eyes. "He still blames ye for that day, ye know."

"Me? What did I do? I was merely a bystander."

"You, my lord, don't know the meanin' of the word. But I suppose ye didn't plan for what happened, so I guess you're tae be forgiven."

"How gracious. So how is Kerry these days?"

"As serious-faced as ever," she replied with a sigh. "I don't think he knows how tae smile. Surely all the angels in heaven would stop singing and the world would come grindin' tae a halt if he ever did."

Derek laughed. "That sounds like Kerry. I always wondered what life had done to make him so miserable."

Megan shrugged. "I think he just has a lot weighin' on his shoulders. Problem is, he doesn't know how tae balance it very well. Not like you—it seems as though nothing bothers you. You're always out in the yard playin' with the village bairns, tossin' balls tae the lads and cartin' the lasses on your shoulders. Never seen a grown man enjoy the wee ones so much. Ye are a prime one indeed—but don't let that bloat your head now."

"I wouldn't dream of it."

"Good," she said, pushing out of her chair and prowling about his office. "As for Kerry, I think he believes he won't be taken seriously if he doesn't act serious." Circling Derek's globe, she ran her fingertips along the top and glanced at him. "Perhaps ye can talk tae him?"

"Oh, no." Derek shook his head. "Leave me out of that."

"For me?" She gave him a practiced moue. Obviously she had been attending the school of feminine wiles while he had been away.

Pouting or not, Derek had never been good at denying her anything. "Fine," he agreed with a resigned sigh. "But if he attempts to knock my teeth down my throat I may return the favor."

"I'll make sure he's on his best behavior."

Derek doubted the man knew the meaning of "best behavior." If not for a begrudging softness his sister brought out in him, Kerry Trelawny would not have a single redeeming quality.

But Megan had that effect on everyone. Her feistiness was infectious—though there was one person it had never managed to win over. Ethan became positively lethal around her, and the only time Megan frowned was if Ethan was in the vicinity.

It was unfortunate that the two had never acquired a liking for one another; something told Derek that Megan would whip his half-brother into shape. But the pair had barely been able to tolerate each other since they were children, exchanging glares whenever their paths crossed.

Derek clearly recalled the day his brother decided it was his duty to shake Megan from her tomboy ways by kissing her under a pine tree, a mistake that nearly changed Ethan from a stud to a gelding.

"So?" Megan prompted.

Derek quirked a brow. "So?"

"Don't be coy, ye naughty man. I want tae know about her."

"Her who?"

"The English miss." Megan tipped her nose skyward and pretended she had a teacup in her hands. Lifting a pinkie, she put it to her lips and fluttered her eyes like batwings.

"You look ridiculous."

Megan treated him to an unladylike snort. "As does she, I suspect."

"She doesn't drink her tea like that."

"Ah, and what else have ye' been payin' attention to, might I ask? And don't think I didn't notice that ye cleverly changed the subject earlier. I'm too wily tae be tricked."

"Indeed you are." He *had* purposefully changed the subject. Rosalyn was not a topic he wished to discuss, especially since he couldn't quite figure out what to do.

"Stop your hemming and speak," Megan prodded. "I want tae know everything."

Something told him this interrogation would be thorough and lengthy.

With a resigned sigh, he said, "Fire at will."

Thirteen

Rosalyn regarded her reflection in the long oval mirror in her bedroom. She had thought that she might look different now that she was officially a mistress, but while the face looking back at her was somewhat wan, she appeared the same girl that she had been the day before.

She took her time dressing, eating her breakfast in her room while preparing herself to face Derek after their night of lovemaking. Wonderful lovemaking, she amended, the memory bringing a shiver to her skin.

Derek had been gone when she awoke, and though she knew this was for the best, she had felt oddly hurt. When he had not been bringing her body to the heights of ecstasy last night, he had cradled her in his arms and they had talked about their lives.

She had learned how Derek had acquired the small scar on his forearm when he caught himself with a fishing hook when he was eight, and he discovered her penchant for wearing men's breeches when no one was looking. He had vowed to pilfer a pair for her from his stableboy, who was about her size.

Derek made her feel safe; Rosalyn wished she could do the same for him. They had not spoken about the incident that had taken place in the east corridor. Derek had accused his brother, and while Rosalyn could see how much Ethan enjoyed goading Derek, she had also glimpsed hurt in Ethan's eyes. Even if she had read Ethan wrong, he couldn't have bashed Derek on the head and been at her bedroom door at nearly the same time, could he?

Something wasn't right. She could feel it in her bones. Several times the day before she had felt eyes on her, only to turn and find no one there. Yet the sensation remained.

But enough of that. She had to stop hiding in her room and face Derek. She had to know if he felt differently about her now that they had been intimate.

She opened her bedroom door and headed down the corridor. The surroundings had all been a blur the day before. Now she took a moment to admire it all.

Some might find the walls dark and spartan, but she saw the history behind the ceiling-high tapestries. Though faded over the years, they were amazing works of art. Battle-axes and shields with clan insignia showed Scottish pride and honor, characteristics so strong in Derek. Rosalyn could see in his eyes how much Castle Gray and its people meant to him.

She felt a stab of heartache for the loss of her own family.

Her mother had mentioned a great-aunt once. Perhaps the woman was still alive? She would be very old if she was, but she might enjoy having a relative around to keep her company in her twilight years. Rosalyn could offer her services as a companion; many unmarried women had such a life. In time she would forget about Derek. Forget about how he had made her body thrum and her heart do strange, wonderful things.

"Such heavy thoughts for so early in the morning."

Startled, Rosalyn found herself face to face with Ethan. She had been subjected to his wild ways more than once, but she didn't think he meant any harm by his antics. Sometimes he seemed genuinely lonely. It had to be hard being an outcast.

"I frightened you, I see," he said, seeming apologetic. "I didn't mean to. I thought you heard me coming. My brother is fond of telling me I tromp like an elephant."

"I was absorbed in the artistry of this wall hanging. Is it Flemish?"

Ethan eyed the tapestry with obvious distaste. "Scandinavian, thirteenth century. It was given to one of my ancestors as a gift by some member of royalty. If it were mine, I would use it as a horse blanket. But alas, Derek has an unnatural fondness for the thing—probably because I loathe it. Anything to irritate me, you know."

"Do you really believe he devotes that much time to this animosity you two share?"

"The man does have other pursuits, like women. He really is quite fond of them."

Had Ethan intended his comment to be a direct hit, he would have been dead on. Rosalyn suspected females flocked to Derek, but he had told her there was no other woman in his life, and she had believed him.

"Frankly," Ethan went on, "the least of his concerns are this house and his people. Yet for reasons I'll never understand, the latter adore him, the little sheep."

Rosalyn didn't believe the bitterness in Ethan's voice was directed entirely at Derek. "Have you ever considered that if you liked the villagers more, they might like you more in return?"

Ethan scoffed. "Why do I care if those filthy cretins like me? They have no impact on my life."

"But obviously Derek does, or you wouldn't feel the need to continue the hostility."

A glimmer of anger passed briefly over his face before his lips tipped up in his patented half-grin. "Was that your kind way of telling me I've become a boor? I agree wholeheartedly. Why I insist on talking about the lad, when I've got you all to myself, is a mystery for the ages."

He unexpectedly took hold of her hand and lifted it to his lips. "Forgive me," he murmured as he lightly kissed the back of her hand. "I'd like to show you how well behaved and charming I can truly be. Would you like to see the stables? They are impressive, mostly because I've had a hand in the development. Our horses are the best around. You may choose whichever mount you'd like, and we can take a ride."

His offer was surprisingly tempting, mostly because Rosalyn felt less sure about seeing Derek. She couldn't shake the unwarranted feeling of hurt. It was ridiculous to worry about the life he had led before he met her.

Derek owed her no fidelity, and she must never believe that he did. She had offered herself to him without demands for a commitment; now she had to play by the rules she had set forth. Which meant that she could not put off seeing him.

"Thank you for the invitation," she told Ethan, "but I'll have to decline for today." She tried to extract her hand, without success.

"My brother awaits, does he?"

"Yes. There are things we must discuss."

"I understand." But instead of letting her go, he took a step closer, his legs brushing the skirt of her day dress. "I hope that you'll give me a chance to show you my better side. I do have one."

"I never doubted it."

He laughed softly. "You are a delight, my girl. The general consensus is that I'm the spawn of Satan."

"I have a feeling you've fostered whatever bad reputation you have."

He rubbed his thumb along her palm. "You are perceptive. I have done most of what I'm accused of."

"And did you hit Derek over the head last night? Should that incident be laid at your doorstep?"

His smile vanished. "No, I had nothing to do with what happened to Derek. Clearly he has other enemies. Not everyone loves his connection to England."

Rosalyn knew there was a serious dislike for all things English in Castle Gray, and she didn't delude herself into thinking that she was welcomed with open arms.

"I hope I haven't disturbed you," Ethan said, touching her lightly on the arm. "Not everyone here has issues with England and her people. In fact, I feel quite blessed to be with one of them."

"That's very kind of you. But you needn't feel you must protect me from the truth; people have a right to their opinion."

"No matter how misguided?"

"No matter. Now, if you'll excuse me? I must go."

"I will escort you. People have been known to get swallowed up in these endless hallways. Some of them haunt this place, doomed to wander aimlessly for all eternity, their remains turning to dust in some long-forgotten corner."

Rosalyn laughed as they proceeded down the hallway. "You do have a sense for the dramatic."

Ethan had not lied when he said the castle consisted of a maze of connecting corridors. It was a wonder anyone found their way.

Ethan suddenly turned toward the wall and touched a small, nearly unnoticeable panel, which, to her amazement, sank inward. In the next moment a hidden door, carved expertly into the stone, opened up to them. A person could walk right past it and never know it was there.

"Don't be afraid," Ethan said as he ushered her into the dim passageway.

"Where are we going?"

"You'll see."

The path was too narrow for them to walk side by side, so Ethan fell in behind her, his hand at her back to guide her. Damp earth and darkness surrounded them. The feeling of being trapped amid the gloom rose inside her.

Rosalyn was on the verge of turning and running back the way they had come when she saw a bright wash of sunlight at the end of their fifth corner.

A minute later, they entered a rotunda. The circular room was ringed with portraits of people Rosalyn assumed were Derek's ancestors. A golden haze pooled on the highly polished wood floor from the rays above.

A domed ceiling soared high overhead, into which an open area was carved, letting in the outside light. Rosalyn could envision the beauty of moonlight coming through that small sphere, spreading a silver glow on the floor, which, she noted, had an intricate design at its center, inlaid in different wood tones.

"There was once an altar in the center of the room, where that design on the floor now is."

"An altar for what?"

"Sacrifices," he replied without hesitation.

"*Sacrifices?*"

"Animal," he explained, "and perhaps some human, as well. This was once a chamber for a secret cult who used it to perform rituals. Pagans who did not believe in God. Lady Emmaline ordered it be sealed."

"I can't say I blame her. It's a horrible thing to immortalize."

"Derek isn't overly fond of this room, either; he's always been a bit squeamish. Anyway, secret rooms demand secret passageways. My father only confided the whereabouts to a select few; he thought it amusing to show guests."

"And you were among the select few?"

"God, no. The old goblin wouldn't have spat on me, let alone relayed such a juicy tidbit. I was a bit of an eavesdropper in my youth."

Ethan shrugged. "I'm surprised Derek didn't have the passageway sealed after his father expired. He probably forgot about it, and I don't intend to remind him. I like coming here once in a while."

"Why did you bring me?"

"I thought you might enjoy seeing something that few people are privy to. And perhaps I wanted a few more minutes of your time. Was that wrong?"

There was definitely a bit of the scoundrel about Ethan, but she couldn't shake the image of the young boy who had been made to pay for his mother's sins.

"No," she said. "But I really must get going. It's getting late."

"And Derek will wonder where you are," he finished for her, an edge to his tone. "I understand." He hesitated. "Will you answer one thing for me before we go?"

"Of course," Rosalyn replied.

"Do I have a chance with you? I mean, is there any room in your heart for me? Or is my brother already firmly entrenched?"

"I'd like to have you as a friend, if that's possible."

"Well, if I can't have you as my own, I'll have to settle for friendship. It isn't as though I have so many friends that I can spare someone I actually like."

Rosalyn smiled. "You know my opinion on that."

"Yes, I'm hindered only by my own abrasive personality. Well, I had best get you to Derek. Wouldn't want to keep the old boy waiting too long. Not a pretty sight."

Within minutes, they had exited the passageway and were back on their original path. Rosalyn could hear Derek's voice as they neared his office. The door was slightly ajar, and the sound of a woman's tinkling laughter floated out, making Rosalyn's steps falter.

She drew to a halt outside the door, spotting Derek sitting behind a chair, facing away from the hall. His gaze was trained on the person who remained just out of Rosalyn's sight.

"Ye should have seen Malcolm!" a female voice trilled. "Ye'd think the ninny would know by now not tae be upsettin' the rooster, since the daft thing is all sorts of ornery. The cock flapped back and forth around the chicken coop, peckin' and squawkin' and makin' a fine racket. Malcolm screamed bloody murder as he ran from it as though he was bein' pursued by the grim reaper himself. 'Twas a sight to see."

Derek joined her laughter, and the deep, resonating sound made Rosalyn heartsick. Could the woman be one of the horde that Ethan claimed Derek had?

"Who is that?" she asked, unease settling in the pit of her stomach.

"That's Megan Trelawny," Ethan replied. "Derek's betrothed."

Fourteen

Derek was getting married?

For the space of a heartbeat, a crushing weight pressed down on Rosalyn. But just as quickly her anger ignited.

Why hadn't he mentioned that little tidbit before she had given herself to him? He had made such a show out of caring for her feelings, telling her that it might be best if they didn't make love; never once had he said that was because he would soon be someone's husband.

"Are you all right?" Ethan asked, his brows drawn together in concern.

Rosalyn fought to pull herself together. "I'm fine.

I was merely surprised. Derek hadn't mentioned his engagement to me."

"He tends to keep it to himself."

The implication was clear; Derek didn't want a potential conquest knowing of his upcoming nuptials.

And yet Rosalyn had difficulty believing that was Derek's reason for not telling her about his fiancée. She searched for a reasonable explanation but nothing fit.

All she knew at that moment was that she didn't want to be there.

She moved away from the door. "I believe I'll speak to him later. If you'll excuse me?"

Rosalyn turned, feeling distinctly like she was fleeing and not caring in what direction she went, as long as it was away from the sound of Derek laughing with another woman.

Ethan's hand around her arm stopped her. "He's not worth it, Rosalyn. Don't let this get to you. Face him and show him you don't care."

But I do care!

How naive she must have looked, throwing herself at him. In the space of one night, she had grown up—and she wasn't sure she liked it. Her dreams had never hurt like this.

Tears sprang to her eyes. She was behaving ridiculously, but she couldn't seem to help herself.

Ethan pulled her into his arms and soothed his hands over her back. "You have me, you know. I'm very fond of you, in case you haven't figured it out."

But Rosalyn could not string Ethan along simply to ease her pain. Blinking away tears, she tipped her head back and looked up at his face. For a fleeting second, it was as though she was staring into Derek's eyes. Both brothers were extraordinarily handsome men, with broad shoulders and eyes a woman could get lost in.

Perhaps it would have been better had she met Ethan first. She knew from the start what kind of man he was, he made no secret of being a rogue. What she couldn't accept was deceit.

"Ethan, I—"

He kissed her, taking Rosalyn wholly by surprise.

She had just managed to twist her head from his kiss when she heard a voice hiss, "Son of a bitch."

The next instant, Ethan was wrenched away and lying on the floor. His hand came up to swipe at the blood that suddenly blossomed from a cut on his lip.

Rosalyn turned wide eyes to Derek. His bearing was rigid and his face filled with fury. He glared down at his brother, his hands fisted so tightly that his knuckles were blanched white.

Ethan stared at the blood staining his hand and laughed derisively at his brother. "Not well done of you, old man. But I suppose that's the way cowards get the upper hand, by striking when one's back is turned. Had you tapped me on the shoulder and asked me to step outside, I would have happily obliged you."

"Get out," Derek growled through his teeth. "Pack your bags and get the hell out of here."

Ethan pushed to his feet and brushed himself off, appearing calm and indifferent. "You're throwing me out? Perhaps you might want to ask yourself why. Then you may want to explain the reason to your betrothed. I think she deserves to know, don't you?"

Rosalyn had forgotten about the woman whose musical laughter had brought such an ache to her heart, and whom she had not wanted to see, or have see her. Now she was left with no choice.

Her gaze slowly slid from Derek, whose brutal regard she could not meet, to the woman standing in the doorway of his office.

She was garbed in a simple dress that needed mending, and her hair was unbound and slightly wild. But none of it detracted from her stunning beauty. Her eyes were green as the Scottish hills, and her face was piquant and impish. Though she looked only a few years out of the schoolroom, she was clearly no child.

"Hello," the girl said, her kindly smile making something fall apart inside Rosalyn. One look in her eyes told Rosalyn she was genuinely warm-hearted; she appeared to have all the qualities a man would want in a wife.

And Rosalyn could not stand there for another second.

Lifting her skirt, she ran past Ethan, who reached for her. Derek bellowed her name, but she did not stop. She didn't know where she was going, but it didn't matter as long as she did not have to see Derek's derision, Ethan's mockery, or lovely Megan Trelawny's pity.

It took every ounce of control Derek possessed not to run after Rosalyn. He didn't know what had made him look toward his doorway in time to see Ethan kissing her. An explosive rage had boiled up inside of him, and he had raced to the door.

Never before had he wanted to wrap his hands around his half-brother's neck and squeeze until he was dead. Yet seeing the bastard kissing Rosalyn, his body pressed hard along the length of hers, all Derek had known was a murderous, encompassing fury.

That fury still pounded through his veins as he faced his brother. Barely controlling the emotions burning his skin, he said, "I expect you to be out of here by the morning. If you so much as glance in Rosalyn's direction, you won't know what hit you."

"My, all this devotion to a houseguest. She *is* just a guest, isn't she? Surely a saint like you would do no wrong."

"I'm giving you to the count of ten to get out of my sight. They'll be no other warnings."

"You forget, your darling mother provided for a roof over my head in her will. Whether it be here or elsewhere doesn't matter to me."

Ethan wiped the blood from his lip with a handkerchief. "That still bothers you, doesn't it? The fact that your mother loved me. I bet you wondered why she cared so much. I wasn't her son, after all. That was your job—or it was supposed to be—but you never really measured up in that regard, did you?"

Derek forced back the urge to lunge at his brother. The bastard had always been able to find his weak spots and exploit them.

What he said was true. Derek *had* wondered why his mother never seemed to hold the same affection for him that she did for Ethan. It had created a chasm between them that couldn't be breached, even at her death.

"Don't delude yourself," he told Ethan tautly. "You were simply a pawn in the war between my mother and father."

"He was my father, too, lad. Don't forget that."

"So your mother said, but we both know she had a problem with her facts. Booze and whoring tends to do that to one's memory." Though Ethan didn't flinch, Derek could tell his barb had hit the mark.

"Your own memory is selective," Ethan returned adroitly. "Even though you like to believe our father's dalliance with my mother was a single unfortunate occurrence, your own mother wasn't foolish enough to believe that. Yet you existed in this contrived world where I was the solitary evil, ruining your perfect life. What you're afraid to admit is that our father could have very well left a litter of bastards dashing about the countryside just ready to make a claim. What will you do then, I wonder?"

"You won't be here to worry about it."

"Please, both of you," Megan pleaded, tugging at Derek's sleeve, trying to pull him away. But the animosity between the brothers had been seething too long, and the volcano had finally erupted.

Ethan shook his head. "Still living in your glass house, I see. Better watch your step, or you might find yourself standing amid a pile of shards. I'll leave you with the quagmire you've created. A rather intriguing dilemma, isn't it?"

His meaning was clear, and Derek could only wonder why Ethan didn't tell Megan. It couldn't be out of regard for her feelings. He was up to something, but Derek couldn't pinpoint what it was.

Megan laid a hand on his arm. "Derek, ye must see tae Lady Rosalyn. She looked greatly upset."

"Yes, brother," Ethan mocked. "You should listen to your wife-to-be. Go console Lady Rosalyn.

I did not force her to kiss me, though I'm sure you want to think otherwise. The lady was willing, and I was more than able. Can you say the same?"

With a derisive grin, Ethan headed down the hall, leaving Derek to seethe and to wonder if what his brother had said was true. Could Rosalyn have wanted Ethan's attention? Could she desire both of them?

Derek ran a hand through his hair, barely aware of Megan as she came to stand in front of him.

"Do ye want tae talk?" she asked quietly.

Derek looked down into the guileless eyes that had always regarded him with trust. He had never misled her; she knew how he felt about a marriage between the two of them, though everyone had propelled them toward that end. His mistake was that he had never clearly dispelled the possibility.

Megan deserved better. He just didn't know what that was at that moment.

"Yes," he said. "I want to talk."

She nodded. "See tae Lady Rosalyn first. Send for me when you're ready." Her smile was wistful as she stood on tiptoe and brushed her lips across his cheek.

•   •   •

Rosalyn stood out in the middle of the terrace, her arms hugged across her chest. Behind her, the French doors that led into her bedroom stood open, her gowns spread out on the bed; on the floor, her trunks were open and waiting to be packed.

The afternoon had passed without a word from Derek. She was glad he had kept his distance; otherwise she might have done or said something foolish. Surely he had to be thinking the worst of her. First she had thrown herself at him, then it appeared she had done the same with his brother. Worse, her shame had to be witnessed by Derek's betrothed.

It was all too much. She had stepped out of one sand pit and right into another. Rosalyn closed her eyes and a tear slipped down her cheek.

She had not allowed herself to examine her feelings too closely, but she could no longer deny how she felt. She was falling for Derek, and out of everything, that was her biggest mistake.

Rosalyn drifted aimlessly across the terrace, stopping at the edge of the cobblestone perimeter to stare up into the night sky. A smattering of stars shined through the leafy canopy, a sliver of moon washing the trees with a silvery coating.

The sound of a twig snapping brought her attention to the woods in front of her. "Hello?" she called out, listening for a reply, but nothing came back to her.

Rosalyn shook her head and chided herself for her jumpiness. It was most likely a small animal finding its way through the bushy undergrowth. She had to stop thinking every strange sound or odd occurrence had to do with Calder. Her stepbrother was undoubtedly still scratching his head, wondering where she had gone.

Even if he managed to find out where she was, the likelihood of him successfully navigating through the rough Highland terrain to find Castle Gray and then sneaking in undetected were slim.

And yet Rosalyn could not contain the goose bumps that rose along her arms as she turned to hasten back into her bedroom—

And into the steely grasp of a shadowy figure.

Fifteen

A scream rose to Rosalyn's lips as large hands gripped her, but her terror died as her gaze collided with Derek's. Her limbs were weak as she sagged against him.

He swung her up into his arms and carried her through the French doors. He pushed aside the gowns scattered on the bed and gently laid her down, then sat beside her, stroking the hair from her face.

Rosalyn felt foolish for getting jumpy over a twig snapping. "I'm fine. I just wasn't expecting to find you there."

"I saw you standing in the moonlight, and I couldn't

resist. I didn't mean to frighten you. When you didn't come to dinner, I got worried."

Food had been the last thing on her mind. "I wasn't hungry."

He was silent for a long moment. "I'm sorry about what happened earlier."

"Why should you be sorry? I was the one who made a proper cake of myself."

"I blame my brother for what happened. He'll be gone by the morning, and he won't bother you again."

Rosalyn rose to her elbows. "I wish you wouldn't send him away."

The fingers lightly caressing her jaw stopped. "So it's true."

"What?"

"Ethan said you wanted him. I didn't believe him."

Rosalyn realized how her words must have sounded. "What happened between Ethan and me was a mistake. The kiss meant nothing—though I would like to be his friend."

A muscle worked in Derek's jaw. "Why? He's a snake."

"He's not as bad as you think. And I just can't

bear the thought of him being banished because of me."

"He should count his blessings that I let him leave with his limbs intact."

"It would be better if I left."

"It appears as though you plan to do just that," he remarked, surveying the open trunks and the dresses strewn about the room.

"I think I should."

"If it makes a difference," he said, "you have nothing to do with the trouble between Ethan and me. I wish I could say my brother has an honorable bone in his body, but he doesn't. I suspect he's just using you to get at me." He stroked a length of her hair between his fingers, admitting, "He's figured out that I care about you."

Rosalyn glanced up. "You do?"

He framed her face with his fingers. "I haven't been able to stop thinking about you all day. You bewitched me last night."

The reminder of what they had done in the hours after midnight made Rosalyn think of Megan Trelawny, and a lump of shame lodged in her throat.

Sitting up, she swung her legs to the opposite side of the bed. "I don't think your fiancée would approve of what we did. Why didn't you tell me about her?"

Derek rose from the bed and came around to her side, hunkering down on the floor in front of her. "The relationship between my clan and the Trelawnys has been strained for years, and my father thought that a marriage between us would create harmony. I never thought there would be any woman who would capture my heart, so I never said no. I just said nothing.

"Megan has never shown any interest in marrying me; we've always been more like brother and sister. But her seven brothers have too much respect for their father to go against his wishes, even though he's no longer living. The only person who might have persuaded them to change their minds was Megan herself, and she's never said anything."

"She loves you."

"She doesn't want to hurt me, I suspect." Derek sighed.

"She seems very nice."

"She is. And she doesn't deserve this from me."

"You aren't the only one to blame. I had a part in what happened."

Derek took her hand in his. "Don't ever think that you are at fault in this. I should have told you about Megan. The truth is, I was selfish. I'm sorry."

"So am I," Rosalyn whispered, rising from the bed and moving around him.

"Don't go," he softly pleaded.

She knelt down to pick up the gown she had worn the first time they had met. She wasn't sure why she had brought it with her; it wasn't as though she'd expected to attend any balls. But the dress had too much sentimental value to leave behind. Rosalyn folded the dress and put it into the trunk.

Derek came up behind her and laid his hands on her shoulders, turning her to face him. "Whether you stay or go, I intend to talk to Megan. And since you've decided that you're leaving regardless, I might as well say what's on my mind. Will you look at me?"

Rosalyn couldn't look into his eyes; she had to get out while she was still able. "Please, just let me pack."

"I knew the moment we left London that I had made the wrong decision in bringing you here."

Rosalyn closed her eyes, hurt going straight through her. "I guess we both made a mistake."

"I didn't say it was a mistake. Just a wrong decision on my part. I knew I wouldn't be able to stay away from you—I found you too alluring and far too fascinating. I took your misfortune and turned it into my benefit. I wanted you here with me, and had Clarisse's missive not appeared that night, I might have been the one crawling in through your bedroom window to abduct you rather than that stepbrother of yours."

Slowly, Rosalyn raised her head to look at him. "I don't believe you."

"I didn't want to return home without you." He took her hand and pulled her toward him. "Stay with me—if for no other reason than protection from Calder. I don't want you to go. Not now."

In her heart, she wanted to stay with him, but she had her own secrets, things that hurt too deeply to tell him about. And even if she did stay, it wouldn't change anything. He needed a girl like Megan.

"Derek—"

He silenced her with his lips, and Rosalyn was lost. He had become a weakness in her blood, and she could not think when he touched her this way.

She clung to his shoulders as he cupped her bottom and pulled her tight, molding her body to his. She moved against him, feeling his shaft swell and thicken with each press of her hips.

He lifted her off the floor. Instinctively, she wrapped her legs around his lean hips. He pushed her skirt back, his fingers grasping her thighs, kneading her flesh.

Rosalyn was so dizzy from his touch that she hadn't realized he'd moved until she felt the cool press of the coverlet beneath her back, the springs groaning as Derek brought his weight down over her, leaning on his elbows to keep from crushing her.

She threw her head back as his mouth sought the sensitive curve of her neck and his hand skimmed up her side to palm her breast, his forefinger flicking back and forth over her nipple, everything inside her aching for him.

He pulled down the shoulder of her dress. The soft cotton tightened across her chest, pushing her nipples high. Rosalyn closed her eyes and arched her back as Derek laved the tight bud, flicking and then circling, over and over again, before drawing the hard point into his mouth.

He toyed with her other nipple, gently rolling the peak until she begged for his mouth, the slightest touch searing straight to her very core, her flesh exquisitely sensitive, heat and moisture building between her thighs.

She leaned up and tugged his earlobe between her teeth as her hand sought out the buttons of his trousers, her palm shaping the length of his erection, her body yearning for the pleasure he could give her.

His fingers wrapped around her wrist and pinned it above her head on the bed, then her other one, allowing her to feel but not to touch.

He shifted between her legs, her skirt pushed up to her waist, leaving nothing but the thin layer of her pantalets to separate them.

He slid a hand down between their bodies and found the opening in her pantalets, slipping a single long finger inside to find her hot and wet. A sizzling jolt rocked her as he eased upward to find the ripe tip of her sex, his stroke like a silken whisper across her swollen flesh.

Rosalyn nipped at his chin and clutched his lean hips with her legs as he took her toward that pinnacle he had so skillfully brought her to three times the night before.

She writhed beneath him like a wanton as his lips moved down her body, suckling her breasts, nipping at her stomach, and she gasped as his mouth brushed her mound and his tongue dipped into the cleft to stroke her clitoris.

She never wanted it to end. Her need for Derek was beyond her power to control as he toyed with the sensitive pearl between her thighs, the little nub swelling and stiffening.

As she was on the verge of falling over that bright precipice, he stopped. He silenced her moan of protest with his mouth while he undid the buttons of his trousers, then slid into her.

"Yes," Rosalyn moaned, loving the feel of him inside her, pumping slowly as he played with her nipples and kissed her softly.

He wrapped his hands beneath her knees and

positioned her legs around his waist. "Hold me tight," he murmured, feathering kisses along her throat, his thrusts penetrating deeper.

She threw her head back and grasped the coverlet, fisting the material in her hands. She strained toward Derek as he pushed. He was in her to the hilt, his cock working up and down, pleasuring her unmercifully.

He shifted her legs over his shoulders, going even deeper. She raised her hips to receive every divine inch of his shaft. It was heaven, ecstasy like she had never imagined.

She moaned and his lips slanted over hers in a heated kiss that should have sent the bed up in flames. He was lust and desire and sensuality incarnate, and Rosalyn couldn't get enough of him.

The pleasure was so intense it was nearly unbearable; the heavy brass headboard trembled with his thrusts.

Her fingernails dug into Derek's shoulders as he rocked back and forth inside her, but they were both oblivious. The only sounds in the room were her whimpers and his low groan.

He suddenly lifted off her, sitting up and pulling

her hips against his thighs so they could both watch as he moved in and out of her.

He grasped the front of her thighs, his thumb dipping into her heat, skimming over the tight, engorged bud that was so exquisitely sensitive.

Seeing what he was doing do her and feeling his rod inside her, his body muscular and beautiful, pushed Rosalyn over the edge.

She threw her head back as an intense climax made her entire body shudder, the deep pulses pushing against him and around him as he thrust once, twice more . . . and then pulled out, his hot seed spilling on her stomach.

Rosalyn closed her eyes, sated and exhausted. Derek reached for the cloth on the bedside table, dipped it into the small bowl of water next to it, and tenderly cleaned her. Then his arms circled her shoulders and hugged her close.

She wanted to say so much, but no words would come.

"Do you hate me?" he asked softly.

Rosalyn blinked open her eyes and found Derek staring down at her. "No, I don't hate you."

He looked so serious that she wanted to soothe him, but she could not. He had ignited something she had never wanted to feel. She had to keep him at a distance.

"I need some time alone to think," she told him. Derek kissed her lightly on the forehead, then dressed. A moment later, the door shut quietly behind him.

Sixteen

Derek stood outside Rosalyn's door, struggling against the urge to go back into her room. When exactly had he lost control of the situation? Had he ever really been in control in the first place?

Forces had propelled him to this end, but whatever those forces were, he was damn fortunate. He wanted Rosalyn more than he could remember wanting any woman, and not just physically.

He didn't want to hurt Megan, but he could not avoid the inevitable any longer.

"Christ," he muttered as he headed down the darkened corridor separating the east and west wings, his thoughts consumed with how best to proceed.

"Bastard," a voice hissed, then something came down on the back of the head, laying him out cold.

The next morning Rosalyn found herself up with the dawn, staring out the window very much as she had done most of the night before.

Enough shilly-shallying; she needed to talk to Derek. She headed out of her room, and at a long, bisecting corridor she hesitated before turning left. She frowned as she spotted something odd on the corner of a marble statue, and bent down to get a closer look at it.

She narrowed her eyes as she reached out and touched the spot, turning her hand to see a wet red smear on her fingertips.

Blood.

She gasped, staring in horror at the statue. Derek had been injured in this very hallway only a few days earlier. Rosalyn told herself not to jump to conclusions, but she wouldn't be able to quell the sickening feeling inside her until she saw Derek and knew he was all right.

Lifting her skirts, she hastened down the hallway, her heart racing, the hairs on the back of her neck standing on end. She couldn't shake the feeling that someone was watching.

She was out of breath by the time she reached the main hall. Normally there were servants buzzing about, getting their daily chores done. Now there was not a soul to be found. The sight escalated her fear.

Rosalyn whirled around at the sound of a doorway opening at the end of the hall. The person was hidden in the shadows until he stepped into a patch of sunlight streaming in through the arched window above the stairway.

"Ethan!" she called in a relieved voice, rushing toward him.

He frowned and stopped in his tracks. "Rosalyn? What's the matter? You look as though you've seen a ghost."

"It's Derek—I think something has happened to him."

"Your imagination is getting the better of you, my girl. He's probably in his office, preparing the guillotine he intends to use on me should I not be gone before the morning meal."

"No," Rosalyn said vehemently. "I found a statue with blood on it in the corridor upstairs."

"Blood?" The smile left Ethan's face. "Are you sure?"

"Yes. Something has happened to Derek; I can feel it."

"I'm sure there is a reasonable explanation. Ah, there's Derek's valet. Surely he'll know where we can find the old boy. Jamison!" he bellowed.

Jamison halted and speared Ethan with a haughty look. "Yes, sir? Is there something I can do for you?"

Ethan tugged Rosalyn along behind him. "Indeed, there is. Where can I find your employer?"

"May I ask why, sir?" Clearly the man didn't trust him.

"No, you may not, you impertinent toad. Just answer the question."

The valet straightened his spine. "I have not seen his lordship this morning."

"When did you see him last?" Rosalyn asked.

He turned to her, his expression softening marginally. "Last night, my lady. He had somewhere to go, but did not say where."

"When was this?" Ethan demanded.

"Around nine."

Shortly before Derek had met her in the courtyard. "No one has seen him since then?" Rosalyn asked, panic building inside her.

"I do not know, miss. I'll inquire, if you'd like."

"Yes, please. Thank you."

Jamison inclined his head to her, then to Ethan in a less cordial fashion, before continuing on toward the servant's door.

"Dawdling bugger," Ethan grumbled as he turned to her. "Well, it seems King Manchester had important plans last night and did not make anyone privy to them. Perhaps he imbibed too much alcohol at the local tavern and is sleeping off a hangover in some alley," he joked. "Or more likely, he hit himself with the statue. The lad has never been the brightest candle on the shelf."

Rosalyn stared at him. "This is serious. He could be hurt, or worse. Don't you care? He is your brother."

"Half-brother," Ethan emphasized, just as Derek had once done. "And no, I'm not particularly concerned about what happens to the sod. If you'll recall, he has requested my immediate departure. One cannot feel inclined to care when one is facing homelessness."

"He was just upset. I'm sure he was going to tell you this morning that you could stay."

"Really?" Ethan quirked a disbelieving brow. "Now what could have brought about such a miraculous change of heart, I wonder?" His look told her that he knew she'd had a hand in Derek's reconsideration.

"Please, you must help me find him."

He regarded her for a long moment. "You really care for him, don't you?"

"Yes, I really do," Rosalyn admitted. "Now will you *please* help?"

Ethan sighed heavily. "Where should we begin?"

Rosalyn tugged him toward the stairway. "I'll start searching the east wing. You look in the west wing. Engage whatever servants you can to assist. Have someone check to see if his horse is in the stable."

"You are a rare gem, lass, and Derek is a lucky man to have you. I can only hope that someday I'll find a woman who will care for me equally."

"You'll find someone. I'm sure of it."

Together, they headed up the stairs. They were halfway to the top when the front door suddenly burst open. Rosalyn swung around, hoping she would find Derek standing there.

"Good Lord, what are *you* doing here?" Ethan

demanded in a surly tone as he stared down at Megan Trelawny, who stood in the middle of the hallway, breathing heavily and staring up at them. "Have your brothers taught you no manners? You're still an unruly hoyden."

Rosalyn noted how pale the girl was and knew something had happened. She rushed down the stairs and took Megan's cold hands in hers.

"What's the matter?" Rosalyn asked urgently.

Megan fought to regain her breath. "Derek," she finally managed to say.

Rosalyn's grip on Megan's hands tightened. "You've seen Derek? Where is he? Is he all right?"

"Aye . . . I mean, no, he . . ."

"For the love of God, woman, spit it out." Ethan came to stand beside Rosalyn. "We haven't all day."

Megan pulled away from Rosalyn and lunged at Ethan. "Ye're a heartless swine!"

"Please control yourself," Ethan drawled, easily restraining her. "I'd rather not have your talons mar this face. Some women find it quite pleasing."

Megan struggled against Ethan's hold, but he would not let go. "The devil will find it pleasing, since that's where ye will go for what you've done."

"Megan, please," Rosalyn beseeched anxiously. "Do you know where Derek is?"

The girl slid angry, tear-filled eyes in Rosalyn's direction. "He's with my brothers."

Ethan groaned. "Her brothers hate Derek. They don't want any man, especially my brother, defiling their darling sister. They were not very happy when their father betrothed the two. I'm lucky I was the bastard of the family, or I would have been sacrificed to this hell-raiser," he grumbled, hitching a thumb at Megan.

She slammed the heel of her boot down onto his toes.

With a growl, Ethan clamped her arms behind her back with one hand and clapped his free hand over her mouth. Muted screeches spewed into Ethan's palm.

"I should have tanned your backside years ago. In case you've forgotten, dear heart, I'm the one man who will not kowtow to your tantrums. Save that for your brothers and my sibling."

"Ethan." Rosalyn laid a hand on his arm. "Stop this. Let her talk."

He deliberated for a moment. "All right, but if

she abuses me again, I'll toss her into the moat." Glaring down at Megan, he said, "Do you understand?"

Her eyes narrowed to slits, but she nodded.

"Good." Ethan removed his hand from her mouth and wiped it on his trousers.

"Derek's in trouble," Megan said. "My brothers have him in the solarium tied to a chair. His head is bleeding."

"Hence the bloodied statue," Ethan said.

Rosalyn turned to Megan. "What will your brother do if we show up at your home?"

"I don't know; I've never seen Kerry like this. When I found out what he had done, I tiptoed downstairs after everyone was abed. I found Derek tied to the chair, a rope around his chest. When I got closer, I saw the gash on the back of his head and blood on the collar of his shirt.

"I didn't know what to do. I hurried to untie him, but I knew I couldn't even hope to move him. Then the door flew open and Kerry was standin' there. He ordered me out. When I told him I wouldn't go, he had three of his men take me away bodily.

"To my shock, Kerry locked me in my room

and wouldn't let me out, no matter how loudly I yelled or banged on the door."

"How did you get out, then?" Ethan inquired, folding his arms over his chest.

"I shimmied down a drainpipe by my bedroom window and ran across the moor."

"Is there any way to get into your house without being spotted?" Rosalyn asked.

Megan shook her head. "My brother's men at arms would see us. It was pure luck that I wasn't stopped. The guard at the back of the house was otherwise occupied." She flushed.

"All right. Then we go through the front gate. We will just have to tell Kerry that we know he has Derek and we want him released. We'll bring all Derek's men, if we must."

Ethan shook his head. "Bad idea. Highlanders take a legion of soldiers appearing on their doorstep to mean a fight. You don't want that. It's better if we go alone."

Rosalyn opened the front door and looked toward the tip of the Trelawnys' castle, visible over the trees that separated one estate from the next.

As they awaited the carriage Ethan had called for, Rosalyn realized that someone must have been working on the inside to have taken Derek unaware.

But who?

Darius appeared in the doorway. "What's all the commotion?"

"Ah, uncle," Ethan intoned. "Here you are in a nick of time to save the day."

Darius blinked. "Huh?"

"Derek has been kidnapped by the Trelawnys," Rosalyn told him.

Darius shook his head. "Not possible."

The coach arrived, and a limber young man jumped down from the box.

"Ready to go, miss?" he asked, popping open the coach door for her.

"We'll be back soon," Rosalyn told Derek's uncle, hoping she was right.

"I'll stay in case the lad returns," Darius replied.

Megan climbed inside next to Rosalyn, and Ethan sat across from them, his arms folded, his expression far from welcoming.

Talking was nearly impossible as they sped over the uneven road that bounced them every which way. Rosalyn held on to the strap above her head for dear life.

"Bloody hell, that boy is going to kill us all," Ethan griped as he saved Megan from falling face-first into his lap. "Can't you stay in your seat, woman?"

Megan's gaze narrowed. "I assume you could do a better job?"

Ethan turned and glared out the window.

Highgate was nearly as impressive as Castle Gray, but not as big, and the view of the ocean was blocked by the woods.

The drawbridge lowered, and the horses' hooves clattered across the wood planks. Noticing the amount of disrepair to the bridge, Rosalyn held her breath until they entered the inner bailey.

The massive front doors of the castle were flung open, and a mountain of a man with fiery red hair and a beard descended the stairs like a bull, six men in full battle gear behind him.

Ethan helped them exit the coach, then leaned against it, looking unconcerned. "And here's the pompous ass himself," he sighed.

"Megan Anne Trelawny!" her brother boomed.

"Kerry, I can explain," she said in a mollifying tone.

He stopped in front of her, his face nearly as

red as his hair as he scowled down at her. "Oh, ye'll be doin' much more than explainin'. Ye nearly did in me and the lads!" He gestured to the men behind him, all equally as big as their eldest brother. "When I found ye missin' and realized ye had gone down the drainpipe, I could have murdered ye with me own hands. Ye could have been kilt, ye little twit."

For such a petite thing, Megan had a huge temper. She jabbed her brother hard in the chest. "Don't call me a twit, ye mutton-headed buffoon. Ye locked me in my room as though I was a child in need of discipline!"

"I won't have ye interferin' in my business."

"This concerns me, too!"

"So ye've brought reinforcements, have ye? 'Twill do ye no good. I'll let the mon go when I'm good and ready, and not a moment sooner."

"Not a good idea, Merry," Ethan said, the nickname causing the ruddy flush on the man's cheeks to scorch a path down his neck. "If Derek's men get wind of what you've done, they'll be at your door shouting for blood."

"And ye think I'm frightened of them?" Kerry sneered. "Ye are no true Highlander, with your fancy English ways. Ye should be ashamed to step foot on Scottish soil."

Rosalyn could tell by the tensing of Ethan's shoulders that the barb had struck home, but his tone gave away none of his anger. "I'll take that under advisement. Now, if you don't mind, these ladies would like to see your captive. If you'd be so kind as to lead the way?"

The laird of Clan Trelawny stood there bristling, his gaze measuring Ethan for a shroud as a muscle worked in his jaw. Finally he said brusquely, "Come." He jerked his head toward the castle and walked away.

Megan's other brothers closed in around them as they were led across the bailey.

Seventeen

❦

*D*ust motes danced in the sunlight as they stepped into the vast stone hall. The interior was dim, unlike Derek's home, where the sun brightened every hallway and room. The castle harkened back to another time, when women dressed in kirtles and the men braided their beards and fed mutton to the hounds whining at their feet.

"Charming," Ethan muttered as they followed Megan's brother down a winding corridor toward the farthest reaches of the house.

"Right this way," the laird said in a smug tone, waving them into a room with a dirt floor and weedy vegetation growing in the corner.

Derek was still tied to a chair in the center of the room, his clothing torn and blood dotting the collar of his shirt.

Rosalyn's temper soared, and she advanced on Kerry Trelawny. "Untie him immediately!"

Megan's brother stared down at her with black, cold eyes, unmoved by her demands. "Ye'll keep quiet if ye ken what's good for ye."

"You can't treat him this way."

"I can treat him anyway I please, considering what he did to my sister."

"What are ye goin' on about?" Megan demanded. "He didn't do anything to me."

"Are ye blind, girl?" Kerry snapped. "Right afore your very eyes, he brings home another woman. He disrespected ye! He cares naught for his pledge to become your husband."

"He never pledged to become my husband! That was Papa's idea, never mine, and certainly not yours. He can do whatever he likes with his life; he owes nothing to me. He never made me any promises, nor I to him."

"If ye were a true Trelawny, you'd never let such a slight go unpunished. Did ye know that your beloved has been sleeping with this woman?" He stabbed a finger toward Rosalyn and said, "Have ye no morals, girl, to be takin' away another woman's husband?"

"Husband implies marriage, and that hasn't taken place. So technically, both parties are free to do as they please," Ethan pointed out.

Kerry swung his pointed finger at Ethan. "You stay out of this."

Ethan raised his hands. "I'm merely stating the obvious. By the by, have you given the old boy any water today? If he dies, all of this effort would be rather pointless, don't you think?"

Kerry frowned, as though he had not thought of that possibility. He snapped his fingers and grumbled something at one of his brothers, who came forward with a pitcher of water. The man raised Derek's head and proceeded to tip the pitcher to his lips. Liquid poured out the corner of Derek's mouth until he started gagging and shaking his head.

"Stop it! You're going to drown him." Rosalyn leapt forward to grab the pitcher from the man's hands, but Kerry gripped her around the waist and lifted her feet from the floor. "Let me down!" she demanded.

"Stop fighting, ye cantankerous hellion," he bit out, grunting when her booted foot connected with his shin. "Damn ye, woman. He's fine. Look!"

Rosalyn stopped struggling to find Derek's eyes open and trained on her. "Derek," she whispered.

"Leave her alone, Kerry," he said in a hoarse voice, "or I'll snap your neck like kindling."

Kerry guffawed. "And how do ye intend to do that lad? I have the upper hand here, and that won't be changin' until you've done right by my sister."

"Blast ye, Kerry!" his sister cried. "Are ye daft? I don't want to marry him. *You* don't want me to marry him."

"I'm protecting ye from shame," her brother retorted stiffly. "Ye should be thankin' me. He will marry ye and make a respectable woman out of ye today, or by tomorrow he'll be dead."

Rosalyn anxiously paced the antechamber she had been put in, a short distance from the solarium. Much to Megan's shrieking protests, she and Ethan had been taken to another room and locked away.

Rosalyn hugged herself and flopped down on

the window seat, which was barren of any cushioning. The room was devoid of all furnishings, in fact, and dust had settled on every curtainless windowsill. Clearly the Trelawny brothers didn't feel any frills were necessary. Poor Megan, growing up amid such a bunch.

Rosalyn only hoped Megan and Ethan didn't do each other in before rescue arrived. Certainly Darius would worry about their prolonged absence and send help?

She didn't know what to think. The word *traitor* kept running through her mind. It was hard to believe any of the loyal servants or members of his clan would plot against Derek. Could this have something to do with her? Caroline had warned her that people would not like her presence, but certainly none of them would have taken their anger out on Derek?

Rosalyn rose from the window seat and paced the perimeter of the room. What was going on? What were they doing? She prayed Derek was all right.

The door suddenly opened and one of Megan's brothers stood there, a scowl on his rugged face.

His hair was in desperate need of scissors, and his cheeks begged for a shave.

"Come with me," he ordered, his manner brooking no disobedience.

"Are you taking me to see Derek?" Rosalyn asked.

He didn't feel it necessary to respond. As soon as she reached him, he took her none too gently by the arm and dragged her down the hall toward the solarium. Relief rushed through her. She would see Derek.

The brother swung open the door of the solarium and pushed her inside. "Sit," he barked, gesturing to a chair that had been placed in the room.

Derek was awake, and her gaze held his as she made her way to the chair and sat down. "Are you all right?" she asked.

"Quiet!" a voice boomed, bringing Rosalyn's gaze around. She had not seen Kerry; her eyes had been on Derek alone. "I'm the only one who does the talking around here, unless I permit ye to speak."

"You always were a gasbag, Kerry," Derek said through dry, cracked lips.

"Ye'll be quiet, lad, or you'll be silenced permanently."

"If anything happens to me, you'll have war on your hands. Is that what you want?"

"I'm nae worried." But he looked worried, Rosalyn noted, hoping it made him think twice.

"Is this what your father would have wanted?" Derek asked.

"Ye'll leave my father out of this. He's long dead and buried."

"He wanted peace between our clans. This is not the way to go about it."

"That's your fault!" Kerry blared. "Ye should have married my sister and not let this tart"—he jabbed a finger in Rosalyn's direction—"distract ye."

"Watch what you say," Derek warned. "I'll tell you this once. Rosalyn has nothing to do with my feelings for Megan. I've always been honest with her. Why don't you ask her how *she* feels? I suspect you'll be surprised."

"Her feelings are of no consequence. My father bade you two get married, and marry ye will."

"Let Rosalyn go. She's not involved in this."

"Oh, but she is. She's taken your affections away

from my sister. Ye've broken the poor lass's heart."

"I bet if you asked her, she'd tell you she doesn't love me."

A thundercloud descended over Kerry's visage as he stormed across the room and leaned down face to face with Derek. "Ye'll marry my sister, ye blighted bastard, or I'll—"

The door suddenly banged open against the wall as another of Megan's brothers entered. There really was no end to them.

"Kerry!" he said urgently.

"What, damn ye?"

"Megan's gone. She's taken off with that one's brother." He pointed at Derek.

"What!" Kerry shouted. "Taken off? Where? We locked her in—Oh, for the love of God. She didn't escape out the window again? Tell me ye had guards posted below?"

"Aye, and we put her in Da's old room to keep her from going down the pipe again."

"So what happened?"

"We forgot that Da's room has the hidden panel." He flushed, which was rather startling on a man of his size. "Megan must have gone through it into the other room and then sneaked down the back stairwell. She's gone. Along with *his* brother," he added in an ugly tone, narrowing his gaze at Derek as though he had something to do with Ethan and Megan's disappearance.

"This is priceless," Derek said with a laugh.

"You'll shut up if ye ken what's good for ye," Kerry fumed. Rosalyn could almost see steam coming out of his ears. "Well," he snapped at his brother, "why are ye just standin' there? Go find her!"

"There's more."

"More what? Speak, fool!"

"There was a note."

"Well, what the blazes does it say?"

The brother swallowed and retrieved the crumpled piece of paper tucked inside his belt. Opening, he read:

Dear Merry,

    I've abducted your sister and intend to have my way with her. She is a luscious morsel now that she has matured and blossomed in all the appropriate places.

And so, merely to spite you, I will take your pain-in-the-rump sister and endeavor to turn her into a proper young woman. Then, if the feeling strikes me, I will marry her.

Farewell for now, old man. Take care of my beloved sibling.

Yours,
The Highland Bastard

Eighteen

*K*erry's roar of outrage resounded throughout the house. It didn't help matters that Derek couldn't stop laughing. Rosalyn caught his eye to silently chide him.

Choking down his amusement, he said, "Well, Kerry, it seems you've been bested."

Kerry's hands fisted tightly at his side. "I've nae been bested, ye filthy devil! I'll find my sister and bring her back before that slimy brother of yours lays a single finger on her."

"If I know Ethan, he'll do exactly as he says he's going to do. So it seems you've gotten your sister married, just to the wrong brother. But you *have* succeeded in uniting our two families, so you've done your job."

"Megan won't be marryin' your bastard brother. That I vow!" He turned to his own brother, who still stood in the doorway clutching the piece of paper. "Send every man available out to search for them—and do not come back until you've found them."

The brother hastened away, and in the distance Rosalyn could hear the sounds of men gathering. She prayed Ethan was far away by now. She didn't want to think about what would happen to him if Kerry's men caught him.

"Kerry," Derek said, bringing the man's gaze back to him. "Before you find my men at your door, I'd advise you to let me go. With all your re-inforcements out looking for my brother and your sister, you certainly won't be able to sustain a battle. End this now while I'm in a forgiving frame of mind."

Rosalyn could tell that Megan's brother didn't want to relinquish the fight, but with a deep-throated growl, he moved behind the chair and roughly undid the bindings.

"There," the man muttered. "Now get out. You've

been the ruination of this family, and it won't be forgotten."

Derek rubbed the feeling back into his arms as he rose from the chair. "Perhaps if you listened to your sister rather than dictating to her, you'd have fewer problems."

Rosalyn tugged Derek toward the door. "Let's go before he changes his mind."

"I've known the man since we were children. He blows a lot of hot air, but he wouldn't have killed me. He was just angry because he had lost control. Megan has always been a handful for him."

"Are you upset about Ethan and Megan?" Rosalyn asked.

"Upset?" A half-grin lifted the corner of his lips as he looked down at her. His face was smudged with dirt, and a nasty bruise was developing around the outside of one eye, but he had never looked more endearing.

"God, no," he said. "I'm not even all that surprised."

"Why not?"

He shrugged. "I'm starting to think that all the fighting between those two masked other feelings.

Megan is a better match for Ethan than she ever was for me. A smile from her could get almost any man to do her bidding, but Ethan was never so easily lulled.

"They are both a hell of a lot of work, though, and I think they'll nearly kill each other before they figure out that they actually want each other. But eventually they will."

He was right. Both were hotheaded and stubborn and didn't give their hearts easily, and they seemed to fit.

She and Derek walked out the front door, and Rosalyn took a breath of the sweet afternoon air. Derek moved to the step in front of her and held her hands. "You came to my rescue. I thought that was my job."

"I couldn't let the man hurt you."

"Why?"

Rosalyn wanted to say what was in her heart, but couldn't. "You helped me."

"So it had nothing to do with how you feel about me?"

"I don't know what you're talking about." He was flustering her, and would soon have her confessing things she shouldn't. "Look! There's Liam."

The stable lad was leading the horse and carriage toward them. "'Tis poorly ill you're lookin', m'lord," the boy remarked, worried.

"I've had better days," Derek replied, patting the lad on the back.

Derek handed Rosalyn up into the coach and followed her in. "I don't relish the ruts we will be traversing. Perhaps you'll allow me to lay my head in your lap? I feel a prodigious headache coming on."

She knew his request was a ruse, but she couldn't bring herself to deny him. She patted her lap, and he didn't hesitate.

When he was settled, he smiled up at her. "How did you know where to find me?"

"I can't take all the credit," she said, stroking the hair away from his face. "I didn't even know you were missing until this morning, when I saw the statue."

He frowned. "What statue?"

"The black marble one in the west wing. I assume it's the object you were hit over the head with."

"Ah, that. I'm getting so used to being bludgeoned, I had forgotten." His expression grew dark. "Someone in my own house wants me dead."

"Do you have any idea who it might be?"

"Not a one. Unless . . ."

"Unless?"

"Ethan. He hates me enough to sell me to the highest bidder."

Rosalyn shook her head. "No, he was just as surprised as I was when I told him you were missing."

"Or he simply acted that way. Ethan has always been a master of pretense."

"I truly don't think he had anything to do with your kidnapping. In fact, I imagine he'd announce it to all of Scotland if he had succeeded in besting you. Besides, what would he have gained?"

Derek sighed heavily. "Why do you have to make so much sense? Let me believe the worst, would you?"

Rosalyn tried to hide her smile as she gently wiped the dirt from his cheeks. "If that's the case, then I don't think you'll want to hear this: I believe Ethan likes you much more than he lets on. He didn't have to come today. You had thrown him out, after all, and he might have been justified in hoping that you rotted in your prison."

"Thank you," he grumbled, playing with the lace around her bodice, a highly distracting tactic.

"I also believe that you may harbor some actual brotherly feelings toward Ethan, though you are both too pigheaded to acknowledge them. Much better to go through life poking and prodding each other than to confess that you don't wish the other to eternal damnation."

"Are you finished?"

"Perhaps."

"May I kiss you, then?"

She had been hoping he would. "You should conserve your strength."

"I've been sitting in a chair doing nothing *but* conserving my strength. I'd like to expend a little now."

"Well, if you really th—"

He brought her mouth down to his and kissed her as though his entire life depended on it.

Rosalyn returned his kiss with equal ardor. She'd been so afraid she would find him terribly hurt—or worse. Deep down, she was glad Megan had run off with Ethan.

They were both breathless when the kiss ended. Rosalyn closed her eyes as Derek feathered his lips over her eyes, murmuring, "I wish you were in my bed right now."

She wished that, too. "We need to see to your injuries," she said instead.

"Bugger my injuries."

She lightly touched his scalp. "That cut is going to need a stitch or two."

"Later."

The coach rumbled to a stop, and Rosalyn said, "We're home." *Home*—the word rolled off her tongue with strange ease.

Derek reluctantly sat up, a beautiful, rumpled sight. Rosalyn could not drink him in enough. He turned and caught her look and gave her a quirky smile. "A mess, eh?"

"An utter disaster. Now, out with you." Rosalyn pushed on his shoulder.

"You're a tough woman, you know that?"

Rosalyn smiled to herself. "If you're well enough to argue, you're well enough to move your two feet down the coach steps. Unless you'd like me to summon Nathaniel to carry you?"

Derek grunted, clearly not pleased that she refused to participate in his bout of self-pity. He exited the coach as Darius came trundling out the front door.

"There ye are!" his uncle said, huffing from his

brief exertion. "I knew those benighted Trelawnys would never be able to do ye in. I wasn't worried a bit."

Derek regarded his uncle with a jaundiced eye. "And if I *had* been done in, what then?"

"Well . . ." Darius's brow furrowed in thought. "I don't know. Guess I would have to take over."

"How convenient," Derek drawled as he brushed by his uncle.

Nathaniel stood gripping the edge of the door as he peered at Derek with wide, worried eyes.

It appeared the boy had been crying, and Rosalyn's heart went out to him. Her heart ached a little more when Derek stopped beside him, beat up and worn to the bone, but smiling reassuringly as he ruffled the child's hair.

"Have you been good today, Nate?"

"Aye, sir." He swallowed and peered up at Derek with eyes full of love and worship. "Are ye all right?"

Derek nodded. "Right as rain. Just a little dirty from my trip."

"Will they come to get ye again?" he asked in a whispery voice.

"Not if I can help it." Derek brushed his knuckles down Nathaniel's cheeks.

Rosalyn nearly cried as she watched them walk side by side, Nathaniel slipping his small hand into Derek's larger one.

She turned to find Darius scowling. "Is something the matter?"

His gaze jerked abruptly to hers, and he regarded her for an unnerving moment. "The lad's too needy," he answered brusquely. "He can't be hangin' on Derek like he does. The man has other things to contend with. But damn if I could get the guttersnipe away from the front door. Must have stood there for hours waiting for Derek to return."

"I think that's sweet. He obviously needs a man in his life."

"Well, it can't be Derek," his uncle snapped and marched away.

Rosalyn stared after him, surprised at his vehemence.

She headed into the front hall to find Derek and his young charge at the top of the staircase. She was about to follow when Caroline appeared from the back hallway.

"Has his lordship returned?" she queried, darting a quick glance around.

"Yes. He's back, safe and sound."

"So nothing happened to him, then?"

"Nothing but a few bumps and bruises."

"I can see to that," she said, lifting the hem of her skirt to start up the stairs.

Rosalyn lightly touched her arm, stopping her. "There's no need. If you would be so kind to bring up some warm water, clean toweling, and a needle and thread, that would be a wonderful help."

Caroline hesitated, then nodded, not meeting Rosalyn's gaze as she headed back the way she had come.

Rosalyn continued up the stairs. She felt sorry for Caroline, and she wondered if Derek had any idea the woman had feelings for him. Her opinion of him would be greatly lowered if he knew of Caroline's feelings and ignored them.

Rosalyn followed the sound of voices, mostly Nathaniel's, down the hallway. His sweet little-boy squeak could be heard asking Derek repeatedly about how he felt and if he needed any help.

Derek draped an arm around Nathaniel's thin shoulders and pretended to accept his assistance, and Rosalyn loved him even more then.

She stopped in her tracks. She liked Derek—but love? Never. She had to remember that.

"Would ye like me to hold your hand while Lady Rosalyn sews up your head?" Nathaniel asked as she stepped into the bedroom.

Her patient was pouring himself a drink from a bottle of whisky. She regarded him in silence until he put the glass down and went to the bed.

"Taskmaster," he grumbled as he dropped his head onto his pillow and folded his hands across his chest, glaring at her like a large child.

"Nathaniel," Rosalyn said softly, "would you help your mother bring the supplies? She should be coming down the hallway any moment."

Nate clearly didn't want to leave Derek's side, but Derek gave him a tap on his rump. "It's all right, lad. I'll be fine until you return."

Nathaniel reluctantly nodded and headed toward the door.

When he was gone, Derek said, "Now, what's that look for?"

Rosalyn put her hands on her hips. "You should be ashamed of yourself. That boy is a wreck."

"What did I do?" he asked incredulously.

Rosalyn sat on the bed and began undoing the buttons on his shirt. "Can't you see the fear in his eyes? He thinks you're about to die."

"I wanted him to feel like he was helping."

"Well . . . do it differently," she huffed, peeling back his shirt to check his chest for any abrasions.

"What's gotten into you?"

"Nothing." Something was making her emotions bubble to the surface. Perhaps she was finally allowing herself to feel the fear she had held back before.

"Ouch," he groused when she probed his scalp. He took hold of her wrist, bringing her gaze to his. Instead of finding anger, his eyes held a familiar softness. "I'll be fine, Rosalyn. I'm not going anywhere."

Shockingly, tears brimmed in her eyes. "I know."

"Today must have been hard on you."

No words would come. She just shook her head and looked anywhere but in his eyes.

She started when his palm settled on her cheek. "It's all right," he murmured.

"You're all bloody." Emotions clogged her throat, and she hated herself for not being the strong woman he had often applauded.

"Rosalyn," he said, stopping her as she began to rise.

She prayed Nathaniel would return and save her from her own shameful display. "I have to get the supplies."

But he tugged her back down next to him. "They can wait. I need you to know that I'm not going to let anything happen to you. I imagine you're more frightened than ever right now. I'm sorry I didn't see it sooner, but I was a bit bleary-headed."

Rosalyn blinked back tears and stared at him. "I don't care about myself. It's *you* I'm worried about. You could have been killed."

"I told you, Kerry wouldn't have done anything to me. But I guess you didn't know that, did you?" He cupped the back of her head, bringing her closer to him.

"Derek . . ."

He silenced her with a passionate kiss. Rosalyn had not realized until then how much she needed his touch and reassurance. She was so very glad to have him there, alive and safe and whole.

Her hands drifted to his chest. His flesh was hot and hard beneath her gently probing fingers, which slid up to his shoulders, kneading the tense muscles. Her body ached for him. She wanted to reaffirm life, to feel his hands and mouth soothing her fears.

When he abruptly pulled back, Rosalyn didn't understand why—until she heard the sound of Nathaniel's running feet, a scant second before he barreled into the room, out of breath and holding the needle and thread, which he proudly held up.

"'Tis the only thing Mama would let me carry," he stated, rushing up to the bed, his intent gaze surveying Derek to make sure he was still well.

Derek lightly buffeted the boy's arm. "That's a good lad. You do know I'll be fine, don't you?"

Nathaniel nibbled the inside of his lip. "Mama said you were too stubborn to die."

It seemed an odd remark, Rosalyn thought, and yet true. Derek was a fighter. "Your mother is right," she said, smiling gently at Nate.

She brushed the hair back from his face as his mother entered the room carrying a silver tray. She came to a stop upon spotting Derek, her face growing pale. Rosalyn thought the woman was about to faint, but the moment came and went.

"What was I right about?" Caroline asked in an oddly chipper tone as she put the tray down on the bedside table.

Nathaniel looked up at his mother. "That the laird is too stubborn to die."

"Nathaniel!" she scolded, a flush heating her cheeks. "My apologies, m'lord. He talks too much. I—"

Derek raised his hand to stop her. "It's all right. I understood what he meant."

Rosalyn reached out and took the tray from Caroline. "Thank you." She smiled, hoping to put Caroline at ease, but got a distrusting look back.

Rosalyn wished the woman didn't see her as the enemy, and it would take considerable effort to remedy that.

"Will there be anythin' else ye'll be needing?" Caroline asked, her bearing rigid as she pulled Nathaniel against her side.

"No, thank you," Derek said.

She inclined her head, and they watched her leave with her son.

Rosalyn glanced down at the needle and thread in her hands. "She cares for you."

"I know. But there's nothing between us."

Rosalyn nodded, wanting to drop the subject. She threaded the needle. "Turn your head to the right, please," she said.

He wouldn't need many stitches, but he would need something to dull the pain. She retrieved the bottle and his glass, and after adding more alcohol, she handed it to him. "Drink this, please."

"Later," he said, guiding her arm to the table, where he plucked the glass from her fingers and sat it down. "Let's just get this over with. I promise I'll be brave."

If he was going to be brave, so must she. She decided to distract them both by talking.

"Have you any ideas as to who might be doing this to you?"

"Not one." He hissed low between his teeth as she pricked him. "If I must rule out Ethan, then I don't know who could be behind it. But I intend to find out. One more clubbing over the head, and I'm bound to be dimwitted for life." It was just like him to make light of the situation. "But there is one thing I know conclusively."

"And what's that?" she asked, concentrating on the last stitch, breathing a sigh of relief as she snipped the thread.

"I know that you are moving much closer to my room. In fact, into the room adjoining mine. I want to keep an eye on you."

"That's not necessary."

Before he could reply, the bedroom door burst open and Darius stood on the threshold, breathing heavily.

"What is it?" Derek demanded, swinging his legs over the side of the bed.

Darius waved a piece of paper. "It's from London," he said in a winded voice. "It's Carew."

His butler? Derek rose to his feet. "What about him?"

"He's dead."

Nineteen

༄

$\mathcal{D}$erek stared blankly at his uncle. "What?"

"He's dead. His body was found in an alleyway yesterday morning."

Rosalyn put a hand over her mouth, shocked and horrified.

"What happened?" Derek demanded.

Darius leaned wearily against the door. "He was murdered."

"Jesus." Derek ran a hand through his hair and stared up at the ceiling. "How?"

His uncle hesitated. "I don't think we should be speaking about this in front of Lady Rosalyn."

Derek turned, and Rosalyn could see how truly

devastated he was. His gaze was blank, as though he had forgotten she was even there.

"This isn't for your ears," he said. "I'll have your belongings moved to your new room." To Darius, he said, "I want her closer to me. There's someone on the loose in this house, and until they are apprehended, I want Rosalyn watched at all times."

Darius nodded.

"You need not treat me like a child," Rosalyn told him. "I want to know what happened to Carew."

"It's not pleasant, lass," Darius warned.

"I can take it. Please finish what you were saying."

Darius looked to Derek, who sighed and nodded. "His throat was cut," his uncle answered flatly.

Rosalyn fought to keep the terrible image at bay. No one deserved to die so horribly.

"His pockets were turned out, but there wasn't anything taken. So the motive doesn't seem to be robbery."

Derek lowered his head and massaged his brow. "I want Bow Street runners, every damn one that's not tied up finding Westcott for me. I don't care who we have to bribe or corrupt." His head came up, his eyes dark and turbulent. "I want them to find out who did this and why."

"Aye," Darius murmured with a heavy sigh.

"And I want Carew's body brought here. He would have wanted to be buried next to his wife." Derek gripped the bedpost, his knuckles white. "Christ. I left him behind to close up the house. He would have been coming here in a few days."

Rosalyn laid a hand on his arm. "It wasn't your fault."

"He was owed my protection, just like you and Darius and Nathaniel and the rest of this clan."

"You're stretched too thin. You can't protect everyone."

"He was a harmless old man."

"You can't bring him back, but you can give him a proper burial and let him rest in peace."

Derek nodded absently. "I want a burl wood coffin. The old codger loved burl wood. And I want him decked out in his finery. I don't care about the expense."

Darius assured him it would be done and left to make the arrangements.

Derek moved to the corner of the room and

dropped down into a chair, his legs thrown out in front of him and his head in his hands.

"What the hell is happening to my life?" he said, more to himself than her.

Rosalyn quietly sank to her knees in front of him, taking his hand in hers. "If anyone is to blame, it's me. These things didn't start happening until I arrived. Kerry wanted your blood because he thought you wanted me instead of Megan."

"I do."

Rosalyn sat back, her hand loosening in his. "What?"

"I've wanted you since the moment I saw you across a crowded ballroom. I was never meant for Megan; forces just propelled us in that direction. I'm tired of fighting it, Rosalyn, and I don't give a damn what anyone else thinks. It's my life, and I want you in it."

Rosalyn was stunned. While her heart soared with his revelation, her mind revolted. She stood up and moved away, staring at the books on his shelf but not seeing a single title.

She heard him rise from the chair and braced herself for whatever was next. His fingers brushed the base of her neck, caressing her skin. She didn't want to respond, yet her stomach jumped as though he had harnessed lightning in his hands, sending sizzling currents along her arms and down her spine.

Her traitorous body ached for his touch; her nipples strained against the material of her dress. Lord help her, she wanted him to smooth his hands over her shoulders and cup her, to ease those beautiful hands beneath the taut material of her bodice and soothe her, then replace his fingers with his mouth.

"Look at me," he murmured, his voice wrapping around her like warm silk.

Rosalyn turned to face him. He was so beautiful. So strong and solid and real. She wanted him to kiss her, and she didn't want him to be gentle. She wanted his passion, every rough ounce of it.

"Please," she murmured, asking for something she could not bring herself to say.

His head descended; her every sense was alive and yearning for this moment, knowing that only in his kiss could she find what she sought.

He cupped her breasts, and she let out a long, low moan as his thumbs swept across the turgid peaks, making her mindless with desire.

She pushed against him, wanting nothing more than to forget all the pain and fear of the day: his attack by the Trelawnys, Carew's death. Her inevitable departure from his life. She knew that he, too, wanted to forget.

A rush of warmth spread between her thighs as he began to weave his sensuous web around her with his mouth and hands. His fingers slipped beneath her blouse and eased the material away, then deftly undid the closures on her skirt, letting it drop to the ground at her feet.

The lace ties on her chemise were next. The soft cotton got caught on her erect nipples as it slithered off her, baring her breasts to his hungry gaze.

His large hands gripped her buttocks, pulling her forward. While she watched through passion-glazed eyes, he leaned down and his mouth covered her nipple.

Rosalyn's knees weakened as he teased the sensitive tip, circling and lapping, her body quickening with each second.

Then he moved to her other nipple to lavish it with the same attention, before taking her breasts and pushing them together, drawing one sensitive nub deep into his mouth and suckling.

Rosalyn thought she moaned his name, but she was so wild with desire that coherent thought had totally deserted her. All she could do was hold on to his shoulders and revel in the pleasure he was giving her.

He dropped to his knees before her and tugged her toward him, pulling her down on top of him on the floor. He kissed her fiercely, his tongue moving in and out of her mouth the way she wanted his body to do.

He rolled her to her back and ducked his head to her breasts again. "Yes," she breathed, as he gently tugged on her nipple while his free hand skimmed up her calf, pausing to stroke the tender flesh behind her knee before resuming the journey along her outer thigh.

She tore at his shirt, frantic to feel his skin against hers. Her fingers brushed the base of his spine, leaving a path of prickling skin as she slowly drifted around to the front to cup him, stroking his erection through the barrier of his trousers, which together they hastily removed.

His fingers swept down her stomach, stopping only long enough at her pelvis to make her wild with anticipation. Then he delved into her heat.

The first touch of his finger against the distended pulse point made Rosalyn cry out with pleasure. Flames of excitement poured through her veins as he massaged her, his mouth creating a warm, wet path between her breasts.

Her nails dug into his shoulders. "Derek . . ."

"Yes, love." His finger slowed to torturous circles. She wanted him to stroke her faster, but he wanted to torment her, to tease.

Each time she felt on the brink of heaven, he would purposely ease back, kissing around her nipple, licking beneath her breast, making one taunting sweep with his tongue across the aching tip. Then he would start again, building the tension, the need, until Rosalyn thought she would disintegrate.

Derek understood her need; he felt on fire with it. It felt as though an eternity had passed since he had last been with her. She made him feel hungry, hot, wanting her with him all the time, and uneasy when she was not.

She gripped his hair as he sank down between her thighs, teasing the swollen pearl with the tip of his tongue. She arched up, crying out his name, her hands gripping his head as he pushed tighter against her, taking the wet tip into his mouth and sucking as his hands cupped her breasts and teased her nipples, matching the rhythm of his tongue on her throbbing clitoris until he felt her entire body tighten and convulse.

His desire for her raged through his blood, searing his very skin. He gave her only a moment to recover before settling between her thighs, needing to tell her with his body what he felt in his heart.

She closed her eyes and released her bottom lip, allowing an erotic sigh to whisper forth. Derek caught the sound with his mouth. Sweat broke out on his body as she squirmed beneath him, the tight points of her nipples teasing his chest as he held his weight on his arms.

She moved her hips in opposing friction to his. He slowed down to prolong the building fever, wanting her next release to be long and deep, as deep as he ached to go inside her.

The thought made him half crazy with desire. He increased his pace and dipped his chest lower, so her nipples would make better contact to increase her pleasure.

He heard her whimpers, felt her writhe beneath him. Her muscles tightened around him like a glove. He lifted her hips and wrapped her legs around his flanks, which brought him deeper inside her.

He rocked her, his thrusts growing frenzied, his body in the throes of a lust so strong it was near to anguish. He forced himself to slow, easing out of her entirely in the next moment.

A protest sprang to her lips, but then he began to massage the nub between her dewy folds with his shaft as he sucked on her nipples, rapidly taking her to that bright, spiraling place once more.

She cried out with her second release, her nails digging into his back as he drove into her, his hands gripping her buttocks, pulling her tighter against his groin as he plunged and plundered, her convulsions squeezing him, his body shuddering as he finally found his own release.

The muscles in his arms shook as he held himself there, lightly kissing Rosalyn's shoulder. He gently eased out of her and dropped down onto his back beside her, his hand reaching for hers, their fingers entwining.

Rosalyn allowed herself to enjoy those moments, believing that perhaps things would turn out the way she hoped. There was no reason they could not go on the way they were, as friends and lovers.

Yet her heart was becoming more and more involved. Even now, if she left, a piece of her would stay in Scotland with Derek.

But did she have to deny herself a few more weeks? Lose moments like they had just shared? She would ache as badly now as she would then, so why not enjoy a short while longer with him?

"Marry me, Rosalyn."

Rosalyn sat up and stared down at him, certain she had not heard what she thought. "What did you say?"

"I asked you to become my wife. I'm sure this is not how you envisioned being asked, but the words would not be stopped."

Rosalyn's throat closed up; she felt as though she were suffocating. Frantically, she reached for her discarded clothing, praying she could get out before he said anything else.

Derek grabbed hold of her arm as she pushed to her feet. "Where are you going?"

"I can't talk about this."

"Is it too soon? Is that the problem?"

Rosalyn could barely shake her head. "I told you, marriage isn't for me."

"But you never said why."

"I did."

"You didn't, and I want to know. I think I deserve that from you."

He did, but she couldn't bring herself to tell him. She wanted to believe that no matter what, nothing would make him change his mind or his feelings—but the truth would.

"I knew you were the one for me the first time you looked into my eyes," he told her. "I don't understand how it happened. I figured I'd be able to spell out every reason why I loved someone, if I ever did, but it didn't happen that way."

Rosalyn refused to believe him. She couldn't. "This is about Calder, isn't it?"

A scowl gathered between his brows. "What are you talking about?"

"You think that by marrying me, you'll be able to better protect me."

"I *will* be able to protect you better, that's true. Then Westcott can't fulfill his plan to marry you and kill you for your money. If I had been smarter, I would have thought of it a long time ago. But that's not what prompted me to ask, Rosalyn. I don't have to marry you to keep you safe, and this isn't some sacrifice, if that's what you're thinking."

Rosalyn stepped away from him. "I don't believe you. You only brought up marriage after hearing about Carew. You feel guilty. That's all this is."

"You don't actually believe that?"

Rosalyn closed her eyes. "Please . . . let's just leave things as they are."

Derek tried to pull her into his arms. "Rosalyn, listen to me."

Angry tears rushed to her eyes. "I won't marry you! I don't love you. Do you understand? I don't love you!" She jerked from his grasp and spun away, ignoring his demands to come back as she fled out into the hall, running until she found herself outside.

There, she dropped down on a bench and cried.

Twenty

For the next two days, Rosalyn avoided Derek, refusing to move into the room next to his and spending much of her time in her room.

Both evenings she had seen Derek appear outside after dinner, which she had taken in her room. She would stand behind her curtains, her heart racing madly. He would stare directly at her window, knowing she was there watching him.

Eventually he would leave, and she would sag against the wall, feeling as though every ounce of energy had been drained from her.

A knock sounded at her door, startling Rosalyn from her thoughts. "Come," she called out.

The young maid who helped her dress stood on the threshold, appearing meek and ill at ease.

"Yes, Margery?"

"Sorry to be interruptin' ye, m'lady, but his lordship wanted me to tell ye that Carew's casket has arrived. He's puttin' it in the chapel, if ye'd like to pay your respects."

Rosalyn had spotted the chapel the day after her arrival, when Derek had taken her for a stroll along the parapets.

"Thank you, Margery. I'd like that."

"His lordship said he'd take ye, if ye like."

"I think it's best if I pay my respects alone."

"Aye, mum." She nodded and backed out of the room.

Rosalyn gathered up her shawl. The days had grown colder as the fall winds moved over the Grampians, and she did not have the proper garments.

But soon she would be on her way back to London. Clarisse had written her, hoping they could spend some time at her country estate in Hampshire.

A few months of quiet in the slower-paced environment outside London would do her a world of good. It would give her time to put memories behind her and figure out what she would do next.

The corridors had become more familiar to her, and soon she was outside. She lifted her face to the late-afternoon sun.

She walked toward the chapel, trying not to notice the curious looks the villagers sent her way. At least they weren't all glaring at her, as they did when she'd arrived. They clearly didn't know what to make of her. Rosalyn didn't know herself. Was she a houseguest? Mistress? Or simply an interloper they wished gone?

Within moments, she spotted the hill cresting the east side of the castle. Rosalyn paused to admire the old church, the spire rising like a long finger into the sky, the sun descending behind it, leaving a dazzling array of red and pink and gold.

She hastened up the hill, slightly out of breath as she reached the top. The doors were open wide, and she could see the beautiful casket in front of the altar. A myriad of candles had been lit, creating a dusky, flickering glow as Rosalyn entered.

It had been a long time since she had been in a church. Over the past year, the church had become a place of sadness for her, as she buried her mother, then her stepfather.

But now a sense of peace washed over her. It seemed that what she had avoided was exactly what she had needed.

She moved slowly down the aisle toward Carew's coffin. Light from the waning sun shot prisms down through the stained-glass mural behind the altar.

Rosalyn stopped to admire the beautiful winged angel, her face turned up to heaven, a beam of white light shining down on her, her arms upraised as though taking the souls of the dead to where they belonged.

"She reminds me of you," a voice said.

Rosalyn whirled around, her heart missing a beat as she saw Derek standing in the open doorway.

"What are you doing here?" she asked as he walked down the aisle toward her.

"I've come to see Carew."

"But . . . didn't Margery tell you that I wanted to be alone, to pay my respects?"

"I wanted to see you. You've been avoiding me, and I'd like to know why."

Rosalyn turned back to Carew's casket and laid her hand on the closed top. "I've had much on my mind."

"So have I," he said, coming up behind her so close that she could feel the heat radiating from him. "Don't you think we should talk about what happened the other day?"

Rosalyn sidestepped away. "This is not the place."

"Then tell me where it is, and I'll be there. We need to discuss this."

"Why? You didn't have to say what you said the other night—so why did you?"

He regarded her uncomprehendingly. "Why does any man ask a woman to be his wife?"

He moved toward her but stopped when she put out her hand. "Can't you just forget what you said?" she asked, almost pleadingly. "Why can't we just enjoy each other's company until I have to leave?"

"You mean you'd prefer to remain my mistress, rather than my wife? Is that it?"

Rosalyn swallowed the dry lump in her throat. "Yes."

A muscle worked in Derek's jaw. "So that's the

reason you've been avoiding me, because I want more from you?"

She nodded.

He let out a short, bitter laugh. "Bloody priceless. Here I've been artfully dodging the bonds of wedded bliss, and as soon as I meet the woman who could change all that, *she's* dodging wedded bliss."

He raked a hand through his hair and stared off at the stained-glass image of the angel. "Fine. Have it your way."

Rosalyn should have felt relieved, yet she wanted him to retract his words, even though she knew this was for the best.

"Good night," Rosalyn murmured. "I will see you in the morning."

She had only taken a few steps when he said, "I'll see you well before the morning, my lady."

The tone of his voice had Rosalyn slowly pivoting to face him. "Excuse me?"

"Midnight seems a fitting hour."

"For what?" she asked, an uneasy feeling welling up inside her.

"For making love," he replied. "You *are* my mistress, if you'll recall."

He strode down the aisle to disappear into the dusky night.

Rosalyn paced her bedroom for an hour before Derek's appointed arrival. She had sent him a note shortly after she had returned from their confrontation in the chapel, explaining that she had a headache and would not be able to receive him.

His reply came within minutes. He would arrive at midnight, as planned, and would certainly see to her well-being. He would not be able to sleep knowing she felt less than ideal.

In other words, he didn't believe her ploy, and he intended to hold her to her own damning words.

Rosalyn contemplated the idea of meeting him in her most unappealing wrapper and nightgown with her slippers on, thinking that might deter him.

"Not likely," she muttered to herself. He would undoubtedly take her anyway.

The thought made Rosalyn shiver. No matter what else might stand between them, in bed they were perfect together. She could never have imagined the feelings that Derek evoked, how skillfully he could make her body sing. And to her wonder, it seemed she did the same thing to him. It had given her the courage to be even bolder, which had garnered the most amazing benefits.

Fanning her face with her hand, Rosalyn moved to the French doors and opened them wide, allowing the cool night wind to dance across her skin.

She closed her eyes and breathed deeply. A calm came over her, and she knew that she would not deny Derek. She didn't want to fight with him—or fight what she was feeling. She wanted to enjoy whatever time they had together. She would give him memories, just as she would be taking her own away with her.

At peace, she opened her eyes . . . and fell back against the chair, a scream building in her throat as a hand clamped down over her mouth to silence her.

"How delightful. My darling stepsister has been found. You can't imagine how worried I've been about you. But I'm here now to take care of you, so don't fight me. I'm not very pleasant when I'm angry."

As Calder glared down at her, Rosalyn felt her

body grow numb, realizing, as she began to slump against the chair, that he held an odd-smelling rag over her mouth and nose.

Then the world went dark.

Derek stared into the flickering flames in the hearth, his feet tossed up on the desk in his study and a warmed brandy in his hand. To the world he might look like a man well pleased with himself, but inside he was seething and confused.

What the hell was Rosalyn doing to him? Whenever they were together, it seemed like she cared for him, that she wanted to be with him as much as he wanted to be with her. There had been a connection from the moment they met. He knew she was the one.

He didn't want to believe she didn't feel the same way. He was sure there was something she wasn't telling him, something that made her keep him at a distance. But what?

If another man held her heart, why would she have given her virginity to Derek? It didn't seem likely; Rosalyn had too much integrity.

Tonight, he would find out what was keeping her from marrying him.

The creak of the door hinges brought Derek's gaze swinging around. He'd thought everyone was abed, especially this particular visitor.

"Nate?" Derek could see tears in the young boy's eyes.

He moved to where Nate stood, hunkering down in front of him and taking his thin arms gently in his hands. "What's the matter?"

"Are you my father?"

Had the lad speared him with a pickax, Derek could not have been more stunned.

He lifted the boy into his arms and sat in a chair beside the fireplace, settling Nathaniel across his lap and brushing the hair from the boy's forehead.

"No," he replied gently. "I'm not your father, Nate."

Nate stared at him with big brown eyes. "But I heard Mr. Darius say ye were."

Everything inside Derek stilled. "You did? To whom?"

"He was talkin' to Mama. He yelled at her that she was to keep the secret or go to her grave with it."

"When was this?"

"A little while after Miss Rosalyn and Mister Ethan went lookin' for ye."

In all the years Caroline had been at Castle Gray, he couldn't remember Darius even acknowledging her, let alone speaking to her. To Darius, servants and children were neither to be seen nor heard.

Had Nate misinterpreted something he heard? Darius knew Derek was not Nathaniel's father; he had been abroad the year before and after the boy's birth.

"Is that why you're up so late?" Derek asked.

Nate shook his head. "Mama's gone."

Derek frowned. "Gone?"

The boy nodded. "All day. She kissed me on the forehead and told me to be a good boy, and then walked away. She hasn't come back. Do you know where she is?"

Derek was going to have Darius's head. His uncle's job was to keep on top of the things Derek couldn't.

"No, but we'll find her. Don't worry. Now why don't we get you back to bed, all right?"

Nate yawned and rubbed his eyes.

Derek held him close, feeling comforted as Nate dropped his head onto his shoulder. The lad's small fingers gripped Derek's shirt.

The clock on the mantel chimed midnight as Derek strode to the back stairs to return the child to his room. His rendezvous with Rosalyn would have to be postponed, but she would understand. She had grown quite fond of Nathaniel; it was hard not to.

Soon he arrived at Nate's bedroom. A stubby candle burned beside the bed, an unseen draft of air making it flicker. The bed opposite Nathaniel's was conspicuously empty. Where had Caroline gone? And why? Had something frightened her?

Derek gently laid the boy down on the bed, tucking the covers around his shoulders.

"Sleepy?" Derek murmured as he stared down at Nate's drowsy brown eyes.

The boy nodded. "Will ye stay until I fall asleep?"

Derek didn't have the heart to deny the request, even though he was anxious to find his uncle. "Of course."

Nathaniel was trying valiantly to keep his eyes open; he seemed not to want to let Derek out of his sight.

"I'm not leaving," Derek quietly assured him. Just as it looked like the boy was finally asleep,

Nate murmured in a blurry voice, "If I was your son, would ye love me?"

The question hit Derek square in the chest. "I would love you with all my heart, just as I do now. You'll never be alone, Nate. You'll always have me."

Nate smiled as his eyes closed.

Derek leaned over and kissed him, then rose and blew out the candle.

Quietly, he closed the door. If Darius was asleep, he would soon be awake. This could not wait until the morning.

Twenty-one

Rosalyn blinked open her eyes. Her head felt fuzzy, and she couldn't get her gaze to focus clearly on the space above her. Everything was dark.

She frowned, trying to recall if she had drunk anything with her dinner. Her body had never handled alcohol well, which was why she generally stayed away from it. But perhaps her nerves had needed calming?

As she struggled toward consciousness, images began to crowd in on her—Calder standing in her room. Had it been a dream? Her stepbrother could not possibly be within Castle Gray's walls.

Her imagination had been running rampant for

months. She thought she had gotten it under control. Obviously she hadn't, if she was still having such flights of fancy.

Rosalyn tried to sit up, but her limbs felt wooden. She concentrated, but could manage no more than minimal movement before she was hampered.

She realized she was not in her room, not in her bed—and something was keeping her immobile.

Shaking off the cobwebs enshrouding her mind, she forced herself awake. She pressed her hands upward against a hard, unyielding surface, her mind working feverishly. The last thing she remembered was entering the chapel and seeing Carew's coffin.

Reality swamped her.

She was locked inside Carew's coffin.

Panic flooded her veins. She screamed for help and pounded against the lid, the wood battering her hands but not budging, the sound of her terror filling her ears.

"Calm yourself, dear stepsister," came Calder's cold voice. "I was merely acquainting you with your final resting place. I thought you might like a taste of what is to come."

In the next moment, the upper half of the casket opened, spilling in muted candlelight and the scent of musty air. Rosalyn inhaled frantically.

"What have you done?" she demanded in a hoarse voice. Her hands and feet were bound.

Black eyes stared down at her with heartless regard. "I merely substituted one body for another. It was not all that difficult. I plied the old codger with one drink after the next at the local tavern, until he had given me the information I wanted. Then I slit his throat in the alley outside. I knew his bloody lordship would have the man's body sent home. I merely put myself in his place at the last moment, and here I am."

"You're evil," Rosalyn rasped out, anguished at knowing that Carew's body would most likely never be found.

"Some might think that. Certainly you and my father. My own flesh and blood didn't trust me—a shame."

"You gave him reason."

"No reason!" he snapped viciously, grabbing her shoulders as though he meant to shake her. With a curse, he snatched his hands back. "What would you know about it? He treated you like a princess. Anything darling Rosalyn wanted, she got. Your mother ruined my life. She thought she would blot out my existence entirely by having a child, as though the two of them were in the prime of their life."

"They were."

"They weren't! There was no room in my father's life for another child."

"That wasn't for you to decide."

"But I certainly did something about it, didn't I?"

Rosalyn stared at him, horror squeezing her chest as she realized what he was saying. "William?" she said in a stricken voice.

"Yes. Dear, sweet William. He was such an adorable little tot. Such a shame he took a spill off the cliffs. Your mother should have known better than to have left him alone. She should have demanded that my father return to London, where such a thing could not have occurred. She had no one to blame but herself, and she did that admirably after the lad's untimely demise, didn't she? She never quite resurfaced from her grief. It really was too bad."

"You killed him!"

Calder shrugged. "Let's just say he was born under an unlucky star—as were you. Fate really is fickle. If only your mother had chosen Lord Keaton rather than my father, she might be alive now, and you might not be about to die."

"But why?" Rosalyn asked, her mind moving at a frantic pace as the minutes remaining in her life ticked away. He would not be deterred now. She had to keep him talking.

"Why do I want you dead?"

"Yes."

"Had you and your precious mother never come into my father's life, I would be very wealthy. Consider that: young, titled, and bloody rich. Why might I loathe you for changing that? If you can't figure it out, I guess you're stupider than I thought."

"Why couldn't you just accept that your father wanted a new start?"

"Because he didn't deserve one. He had a wife; she died. I was his heir. No one else should have gotten a single shilling. Certainly not you."

"He left you with plenty. Three estates, a working mine, money."

Calder leaned down close to her face, his breath warm and foul-smelling. "He should have left me everything. He sealed your fate when he gave you a trust fund."

"You can have it."

"That's what I intend, my dear. You took me for a fool—that was your first mistake. You had to know I'd hunt you down, and shouldn't have put me through all this effort. Your lover didn't help matters by throwing Bow Street runners on my tail—or his bloodhound friends. They were worse than the law; one actually came close to catching me. I wouldn't be surprised if he has discovered my destination and is closing in as we speak. So I hope you don't mind if I make your end quick. I can't promise it will be painless, however. You *did* cause me quite a bit of trouble."

"Calder, listen to me."

"I'm afraid I haven't the time," he remarked as he extracted a small knife from his jacket pocket, the metal blade glinting wickedly in the light. "Hold still now. I wouldn't want to slip and have to start all over again."

As the knife descended Rosalyn opened her

mouth to scream, but Calder clamped his hand down, silencing her.

"You intend to make this difficult, I see." Using his free hand, he stuffed a handkerchief in her mouth. "Now, where was I?"

The blade touched her throat, and Rosalyn struggled wildly, her cries muted. Calder's grip suddenly slackened, his head turning.

"Shut up," he hissed, his gaze snapping toward the vestibule.

Rosalyn stilled, her heart pumping in her ears. She prayed someone was there. No matter what, she would fight. He would not take her like this.

The casket slammed shut, enveloping her in darkness again. She didn't know if Calder was still there or if he had run off. She listened, desperate for something to tell her she was not alone.

Muffled noises reached her ears, but she couldn't tell what was happening.

Then light suddenly filled her eyes as the coffin lid swung open.

Derek knocked at his uncle's bedchamber, barely waiting for Darius to bid him entry before he threw open the door.

Darius sat at his writing desk, a bottle of port open beside him and an empty glass in his hand. He didn't seem surprised to see Derek.

"Come in, m'boy. Have a drink with me."

"What are you still doing up?" Derek asked, closing the door behind him.

"It's been a rough few days. Gives a man strained nerves."

"And what might be straining your nerves now, uncle? Perhaps your conversation with Caroline?"

"You know?"

"Yes, I know. I also know that she's disappeared. Why wasn't I told?"

His uncle tipped the bottle of port to his glass and filled it nearly to the top. "Ye didn't need any more worries."

"That's not for you to decide. I'm laird here, or have you forgotten? What has happened to Caroline?"

"She's gone."

"*Where* has she gone?"

Darius shrugged. "Don't know."

"And you didn't think to send someone out to search for her? She could be hurt, or worse."

"Nay, lad. She's not hurt. She left because she wanted to. She won't be comin' back."

"She wouldn't just leave Nathaniel here."

"She couldn't take him."

Derek clenched his jaw. "What the hell is going on?"

Darius gestured to the chair across from him. "Sit down. We need to talk."

Derek sat. "All right—now speak. Where is Caroline, and why did she leave?"

"I canna say where she is for certain. Perhaps London, by now, or maybe even on a ship bound for America. She always talked about going abroad."

"I never heard her say that."

"Perhaps ye weren't really listenin'. I heard more than you—it was my job to do so. As your father's right hand, and now yours, I had to know what was goin' on in Castle Gray. I suspect there are many things ye don't know. But none of it was really worth tellin'." He paused, then added, "And there were some things I couldn't say."

"Like what?"

"I had been sworn to secrecy, and I took my oath seriously."

"Who swore you to secrecy? Caroline? Nathaniel heard you tell her that I was his father."

Darius sighed and stared down at the drink in his hand. "I didn't know the lad was there."

"What would make him think I was his father? There's not a soul alive who would believe that."

"I never thought anyone would. But I had not been talkin' about you at the time."

"Then who?"

Darius's fingers tightened around his glass as he looked Derek in the eye. "Your father."

Understanding hit Derek like a fist to the stomach. "Jesus."

"Aye." His uncle gave a weary sigh. "I couldn't believe it, either. First he sires one bastard that he refuses to acknowledge, then he dares bring another snot-nosed brat into this house."

Derek's anger rode to the fore. "Nate better not have heard those words from your lips."

"He never has, that I swear. Caroline was too protective of the boy. But now ye see why she couldn't take him. He's your brother, lad. Your flesh and blood. She knew it was only a matter of time before ye found out.

"I'm surprised ye didn't notice the resemblance sooner. I suspect Ethan did; he always smirked when he saw the tot. I figure he was waitin' to discharge that particular bullet when he knew it would do the most damage."

Derek got up and paced the room. Nate, his brother. Apparently everyone had known the truth but him.

"So why am I the last to know? And what made Caroline think she had to leave? I would never have thrown her out; she had to have known that."

"She did. But your finding out was not the reason she left."

Derek glanced over his shoulder. "What is?"

"I confronted her about what happened to ye the other day, with the Trelawnys. Ye had to be wonderin' how anyone could have gotten in here. It was someone on the inside."

"And you're going to tell me now that person was Caroline? Why would she do it?"

"That should be obvious: because you'd tossed her aside. Just as your father did when he found out she was pregnant. I think the silly gel had some grandiose visions that your father would divorce your mother and marry her, that he would make her son legitimate even though he hadn't done so with Ethan."

A thought Derek had often pushed to the back of his mind crowded in on him. Ethan had once been a small boy very much like Nate, wondering where his father was and why the man didn't love him enough to claim him as his own.

It made Derek ashamed to have William Mc-Dougal as a father, and he hurt for his mother, who'd had to live with her husband's open infidelity.

For years, Derek had secretly harbored resentment toward her, thinking that she had been too harsh and unforgiving to his father. Never once had she tried to make Derek see her side, but he wouldn't have listened anyway. He had been too pigheaded.

Perhaps that was why she had always shared more of a bond with the son that was not hers. Ethan had never judged her. They had both been recipients of harsh punishment, while Derek had lived in his glass house, as Ethan had once accused.

"So," Darius said, finishing his story, "I went to Caroline when Ethan and Lady Rosalyn left to fetch ye from Trelawny Castle, and I told her I knew what she'd done. She broke down in tears and told me that she had to do it—she wouldn't allow another man to use her and discard her. So she'd plotted with the Trelawnys to get back at ye. She was terrified what you'd do to her when ye found out, and she knew that when ye discovered her deception, you'd learn of the lad's parentage. Ye would have come after her to retrieve your brother, so, she left him here to be with ye."

"We have to find her. Nathaniel will be devastated without her."

"I suspect finding her will prove difficult, if she doesn't want to be found."

"Did she have any friends that you know of? Anyone who might know where she might go?"

Her parents, from what he could recall, were both dead, and she had never mentioned any other relatives.

"I'll inquire," Darius said. "I did see her speaking with that timid maid. What's her name?"

Derek scoured his mind. "Margery?"

Darius nodded. "Aye. I'll speak to her and see if there is anything else I can find out."

Derek was at a loss for what else to do. He knew he'd be getting no sleep tonight. It was now after one in the morning, and Rosalyn was surely asleep. He shouldn't wake her, but he wanted to see her.

He headed to the door. "I want to know anything you find out," he informed his uncle, "no matter how minor it may seem. I want Nathaniel moved into the room opposite mine. He's to be watched at all times, I don't want him left alone. And there's to be no mention of this. I will decide what to tell the clan. Do you understand?"

"Aye," Darius replied gruffly.

Derek left. The fact that Darius had kept all this to himself, long after his brother's death, did not sit well with him. There were to be no secrets under his roof. But he would deal with his uncle at the appropriate time.

Nathaniel was his brother! He still couldn't believe it, yet he wondered why he hadn't figured it out sooner.

Nate would have been conceived during one of the rockiest periods in his parents' marriage, shortly after his mother had left and gone back to England.

His father had become enraged and even more

bitter. It didn't seem to matter who he hurt. Caroline had been barely more than a child herself, and knowing her as he did, Derek doubted she would have denied his father.

The old laird didn't tolerate being told no, and Caroline hadn't had anywhere else to go. It was either submit or be thrown out. And Derek had little doubt that was exactly what his father would have done.

Damn the man to hell. He had denied Derek his brother. In a way, he had denied him *both* of his brothers by fostering Derek's animosity with Ethan.

"There you are, my lord! Thank goodness I've found you."

Derek glanced up to see his valet hurrying down the hallway. "What is it, Jamison?"

"Peters sent me in search of you. There are visitors, my lord."

"Visitors? At this hour?"

"They said it was imperative they speak to you. Since the sentry recognized them as your friends, he let them by. I hope he didn't do wrong?"

"Who is it?"

"Mr. Kendall, sir. He's come with his wife, Lady Francine, as well as Lord Anthony Tremayne. They said they need speak to you immediately. They await you in the library."

Derek was already turning the corner toward the main hallway before his valet had finished his sentence.

Twenty-two

※

$\mathscr{R}$osalyn stared up at the figure looming behind the casket, panic making her heart thrum wildly. She geared herself for a fight, but then the person moved out of the shadows and tugged the rag from her mouth.

"Ethan?"

"In the flesh, my girl." He smiled down at her in that devilish fashion he was so well known for. "I see you're in a bit of a spot, but I'm here to save the day." He began undoing the rope that bound her legs and wrists together.

"How did you get here? And where's Calder?"

"I presume that was the person hovering over you a few minutes ago?"

"Yes, but—"

Ethan helped her to sit up. "The man is dead. He came at me with a knife and I felt compelled to return the gesture, but with my fists, as is the gentleman's way. Unfortunately, when he fell back, he cracked his head on the corner of the altar."

He slid his hands beneath her legs and lifted her into his arms. "Did he hurt you? I'd be happy to rouse him from death and kill him again, if so."

"I'm fine," Rosalyn told him, still trying to grasp the fact that her stepbrother was dead. "Are you sure he's . . . ?"

"Quite. I'll show you if you'd like, but it may be best not to have such a gruesome memory for the rest of your life."

"Thank you," she said.

"Completely unnecessary. I live to be of service." He shot her a roguish wink.

"So what are you doing here? I thought you had run off with Megan Trelawny."

"Pray, do not remind me," he muttered. "I came upon your abduction quite by accident. I was on a mission to raid food from the pantry when I heard voices in the courtyard and spotted you being carted off over someone's shoulder. Thinking my sibling had developed barbaric tendencies, and thereby intrigued beyond measure, I followed . . . and here we are."

"What were you doing in the courtyard? And where have you been for the last two days? I had assumed you and Megan were miles away from here by now."

"That was the assumption I was going for—I knew this was the last place the Trelawnys would look. I figured we'd be safe here for a few days until the uproar had died down, then we could sneak away in the middle of the night. Once things had sufficiently settled, I would then send the chit back to the loving bosom of her crazed family and be done with it."

Rosalyn quirked a brow. "Really?"

"Please don't give me that look. My intervention at the Trelawnys' was purely for your benefit."

"I don't believe that any more than you do."

Ethan frowned at her, clearly not appreciating the fact that she had seen through his facade.

"Come inside with me; I'm sure Derek will allow you back."

"A noble gesture, but I'm not sure I want to be

back. Other things await me." Megan, he meant. He *did* care for her.

"Then I guess this is good-bye for now. Take care of yourself."

"And you, sweet girl. Give his bloody lordship a run for his money."

Rosalyn laughed as she headed toward the front doors of the church.

"I don't suppose you'll refrain from telling my half-brother of my gallantry?" Ethan called after her.

"Of course not," Rosalyn replied, giving him a dose of his own medicine as she stepped out into the sweet night air. "Your heroic deeds will be lauded far and wide. Prepare to be a hero, my good sir."

Her gaze set upon Castle Gray, and a sudden yearning struck her. She needed to see Derek, to feel his arms around her.

Lifting her skirt, she ran down the hill.

Derek heard voices as he crossed the foyer and headed toward the library. At least ten different scenarios went through his head as to why his two closest friends were at his house in the middle of the night—none of them good.

Had they found Westcott? Was the man incarcerated—or better yet, dead? Derek fervently hoped it was one or the other, for only then would Rosalyn know peace.

She would also leave him.

Derek shook off the thought. He wasn't letting her go that easily. Once she no longer had the burden of her stepbrother hunting her down, perhaps whatever was bothering her would be alleviated as well.

He stood for a moment on the threshold of the library, regarding his friends. Anthony and Lucien were at opposite ends of the couch, with Lady Francine in the middle. They faced the fireplace, talking in animated voices, unaware that he had arrived.

Lucien, of all people, was now a married man. The last thing Derek recalled hearing was that he had taken Fancy somewhere, and no one had seen or heard from them for over a week. That was shortly before Derek had become entangled in Rosalyn's life.

Then there was Anthony—the youngest son of the duke of Glenmore and utterly content to be a rakehell.

"Good evening, Lord Manchester," a soft voice

murmured. Lady Francine was facing him from across the room.

Lucien surged to his feet and smiled, a look of contentment on his face that Derek had not seen in a very long time. "Good God, old man, you still move like a bloody wraith. Hope you weren't there long enough to hear Tremayne maligning your character."

"Bluster," Anthony retorted, sporting a half-grin as he rose from the couch. "Thank goodness Lady Francine has taken the boor in hand. Perhaps she will succeed where others have failed." To Fancy he said, "You have my most profound sympathies, my lady."

"Bugger off, sod," Lucien growled good-naturedly as he tugged his wife to his side. "The lady adores me." Turning her toward him, he murmured tenderly, "Don't you, love?"

"Without question." She leaned in to kiss him gently on the cheek.

Derek cleared his throat, shaking the couple from their dream world.

A light blush dusted Fancy's cheeks as she looked at Derek. "Is Rosalyn in bed? I don't wish to wake her, but I have missed her so."

"She's missed you as well," Derek replied. "Seems you two have had several adventures."

Fancy's eyes lit with amusement. "I suppose we have."

"Yes, like shooting me in the leg," Lucien grumbled.

His wife smiled patiently at him. "Be glad my aim was off."

"I am supremely glad, love. Otherwise, you would not now be enjoying the bedchamber as you do."

Mortification blossomed on Fancy's face, and she swatted at her husband, who laughed.

"Perhaps we could get to the matter at hand?" Anthony intoned drolly.

"Tell me this is about Rosalyn's stepbrother," Derek said.

"Yes, it is. Two days ago, I got wind of his whereabouts. It appears he's on his way here," Lucien replied.

"He wouldn't make it past the gate."

"That's what we hope," Lucien said. "But we had to be certain."

"Are you sure Rosalyn is all right?" Fancy asked, her worry evident.

Derek's first thought was to say yes, but he had never made it to her room for their rendezvous.

"I imagine she's asleep by now," he answered.

"When did you see her last?" Fancy persisted. "I've had an uneasy feeling all day, and I just need to know that she's all right. Then I will be able to breathe a sigh of relief."

"Come with me," Derek told her and headed out the door.

They went up the stairs side by side. Just before they reached the top, the front door opened. They looked down to see Rosalyn enter, barefoot and rumpled, her hair a wild mass down her back.

Derek took the steps down two at a time and grasped her arms in his hands. "My God, what happened?"

"I'm fine. Goodness, I cannot count how many times I have said those two words since leaving London. But I'm grateful to be able to keep saying them." Her gaze suddenly drifted around Derek's shoulder, and her brow furrowed. "Fancy?" She blinked. "*Fancy!*"

Rosalyn tore herself from Derek's grip and catapulted around him to reunite with her friend. The women hugged and cried.

When the two finally separated, Rosalyn asked Fancy, "What are you doing here? The last thing I heard was that you had gone off with Mr. Kendall. I couldn't find out a single thing. I was so worried."

"I should be apologizing for that," came Lucien's voice as he moved into the hall. "I unfairly commandeered your friend. I hope you will forgive me, considering I made an honorable woman out of her in the end."

Rosalyn's gaze shifted from Lucien back to Fancy, who inserted somewhat sheepishly, "Rosalyn, may I introduce you to my husband?"

Rosalyn stared for a full ten seconds, and then launched herself into Fancy's arms again. "How wonderful! I knew you two were meant for each other right from the start."

"I know I always said you would be my maid of honor," Fancy said, "but everything happened so fast. I do hope you'll forgive me."

Rosalyn squeezed Fancy's hand. "There's nothing to forgive. I'm just so happy you're here. I've missed you desperately."

"And I, you. Now, tell me, what has been going on? Why were you outside, and shoeless?"

"Oh, yes—that," Rosalyn said. Amazingly, she had forgotten what had just transpired. "Well, I was abducted."

"*What?*" Derek bellowed.

"*Who?*" Lucien demanded.

"*When?*" Anthony insisted.

"Again?" Fancy said, the only calm voice in the bunch.

Rosalyn sighed. "Yes, and it grows very tiresome. I have begun to think that I will be relegated to bunking in the breakfast salon if I wish to sleep through the night. My bedroom has become a place one goes if one does not wish to actually sleep."

Derek growled impatiently as he took hold of Rosalyn's shoulders and turned her to face him. "Who abducted you?"

She stared at him. "Why, Calder, of course. Who else?"

"Who else, she asks," Derek muttered, to which Anthony shook his head.

Noting the new person in the group, Rosalyn smiled. "Hello."

"Hello," Anthony replied, returning her smile. "I'm glad to see you back unharmed, my lady."

"Thank you . . ."

"Lord Anthony Tremayne," Lucien filled in. "Ne'er-do-well and occasional philanthropist, as long as the philanthropy is directed at himself."

In the calmest tone Derek could muster, he said, "Rosalyn, where is Westcott? Is he still here or has he run off?"

"He's gone."

Derek cursed beneath his breath. "How could the man have slipped in and out undetected? My men will answer for this."

"My lord," Rosalyn said, trying to get his attention.

"I will see my men doubled. No, tripled! He will not get in here again without a bullet between his eyes—I promise you that."

"My lord," Rosalyn interjected more forcefully.

"I'll hunt the slimy maggot to ground. He'll not make a fool of me again."

"My lord!" Rosalyn nearly shouted, out of patience.

He swung around to face her, a frown on his face. "What?"

The man could be so damn thick sometimes. "I know how Calder got in." She hated to tell him so bluntly about poor Carew, but she had no other choice. "It seems he substituted himself for Carew in the coffin."

"Substituted?"

"He removed Carew's body in London, drilled a small hole for air, and traveled here in his place." In a soft voice, she added, "I'm so sorry. Carew didn't deserve such an ignoble end."

Derek stood unmoving, his face having lost some of its color.

Rosalyn laid a hand on his arm to comfort him. Eventually, his gaze lifted, and the expression in his eyes was murderous. "Where is the bastard?"

"In the church vestibule."

"Did he hurt you?"

"No." It would do no good to tell him of her terrible fright, or the horror she still felt, thinking she would be buried alive. "He merely took me by surprise. The next thing I knew, I woke up in a coffin."

Three pairs of eyes stared at her.

"He put you inside the coffin?" Lord Tremayne asked in a disbelieving tone.

"Yes." Rosalyn forced back a shiver.

"How did you get away?" Fancy asked.

"Through no virtue of my own, I'm afraid. Derek's brother was closer than we all thought."

Derek frowned. "Ethan? What did that blighter do?"

"He spotted Calder carting me off and followed. When Ethan engaged in a fight with my stepbrother, Calder fell back against the corner of the altar. He's dead."

"So where was Ethan all this time?" Fancy queried.

"In an antechamber that he claimed a group of pagans used for secret rituals hundreds of years ago."

"My father had that 'secret antechamber' built when he became laird," Derek said. "He thought it fun to fool people into believing the castle had a ghoulish history."

"Seems your brother has quite the imagination," Fancy remarked, amused. "I should like to meet him."

Rosalyn glanced at Derek. "He is on an extended hiatus at the moment."

Derek turned his gaze to Fancy. "Might I prevail upon you to take Lady Rosalyn back to her room? She needs her rest."

The request, made without any emotion, was a blow to Rosalyn. Derek wanted her out of sight. Clearly she had caused him enough trouble, and he wanted to be done with it.

Fancy nodded. "Of course, my lord."

Derek pivoted on his heel, then stalked to his office and closed the door soundly after him.

Twenty-three

Derek wrenched the stopper from the brandy decanter. Instead of pouring the standard two fingers, he went for four. Then five. He downed half of the potent brew in his first swallow and closed his eyes.

He had almost lost Rosalyn tonight. His inability to protect her had nearly cost the woman he loved her life—and it had all happened beneath his very nose, with him none the wiser.

He had been so sure he could save Rosalyn from any danger that presented itself, but when the time came to prove it, it had been Ethan who saved her. Ethan, who had saved Megan.

Ethan, who had saved Derek himself.

•   •   •

Rosalyn stared out the same window that Derek had so recently stood in front of. What had he seen when he looked out into the dark void of the nighttime sky? The same emptiness she now saw? An emptiness that matched what she felt inside?

What was to keep her here now? Calder was dead. She had been hunted for so long, and then in minutes, the threat had been eliminated. She had lived under that threat for so long, it was hard to believe it no longer existed.

Now she had to face the real reason she had to leave: she loved Derek. He had walked out of her dreams, her fantasies, and into her life and heart. He deserved a woman who was whole, not one who was barren.

Scarlet fever had left her without the ability to have children, and no man would accept that? Men wanted heirs to continue the family line.

Fancy came to stand beside her, laying a hand on her shoulder. "Are you all right?" she asked.

"Just tired." Her thoughts would not let her be.

"Our lives are changing."

"I know. It seems like yesterday when we were scaling the rocks at Meadow's Cove," Rosalyn said.

"Or following seagulls down the beach."

"We've grown up."

"It seems we have," Fancy murmured. "It's a bit frightening."

"You've never been scared a day in your life. That's my territory."

Fancy cocked her head, an incredulous look on her face. "You don't actually believe that? I've been scared more times than I care to admit."

"I've never seen it."

"Because I didn't want the world knowing what a coward I am."

"You?"

Fancy nodded. "I wish it weren't so, but it is. I never realized how frightened I was until Lucien came into my life. I had built a wall around myself after my parents died, refusing to look at things for what they were. It got worse when Grandmother and George passed away. I felt so alone, so helpless. But I had you," she said with a smile, squeezing Rosalyn's hands. "You were my salvation."

"And you were mine."

"And now you're free."

But what exactly did her freedom give her?

Pulling Rosalyn toward the bed, Fancy sat her

down. "Why don't you tell Derek how you feel? You can't deny it, it's in your eyes. And Derek's."

Rosalyn glanced down at her hands. "A relationship between us is not possible."

"He's an available man, and you're an available woman."

"But I'm not a whole woman!" Rosalyn cried.

Fancy sighed. Loudly. "Good Lord, Rosalyn, tell me you aren't going to base your future on something that may or may not be true. You may very well be capable of carrying a child. Many children, in fact."

"But the doctor—"

Fancy waved a dismissive hand. "He was probably an old coot who brandished some textbook theory he'd learned in *his* youth. Have you ever spoken to a doctor since then?"

"No."

"For all you know, you could be fertile."

Rosalyn cautiously considered the possibility. "But what if I'm not?"

"Then there are plenty of orphaned children who would feel blessed to have such a loving mother. And any man who loves you—truly loves you—would stand beside you."

Perhaps that was what Rosalyn feared even more than being barren; that the man she chose to love didn't love her enough in return. She was afraid of taking that chance.

"Think about it, won't you?" Fancy quietly asked. "Your happiness means more to me than anything."

"As does yours to me. Is Lucien making you happy?"

Fancy's eyes sparkled. "I'm thoroughly in love with my husband. I have to pinch myself every day to make sure I'm not dreaming." She took Rosalyn's hands. "And I wish that same love for you. Believe in yourself as I believe in you."

Fancy nodded and watched her friend leave, wishing beyond measure that she could have what Rosalyn had: a love that would last a lifetime.

Derek stared into the dying fire and listened to the clock on the mantel chime three in the morning. Even with several glasses of brandy in him, he was unable to sleep. His mind kept drifting to images of Rosalyn.

The way she had looked the night they first

met, dressed in a lemon-hued chiffon gown that could not equal the sunshine of her smile.

The way she laughed when she was riding a horse full out.

How her eyes lit up whenever she spoke of her parents or Lady Francine.

And the way those eyes looked at him when he was making love to her, as though he was the only man in the world, setting his soul on fire.

The creak of a floorboard brought Derek swinging around in his chair. A figure emerged from the shadows. "Rosalyn?"

She was dressed in a wrapper over her nightgown. Her beautiful face held a look he could not interpret. He rose from his chair.

"Are you all right? Has something happened?"

Rosalyn shook her head. She had rehearsed what she had wanted to say, knowing the only way she would make it through was if she had her speech memorized.

But now that she was here with Derek, she wanted one more touch, one more taste of his mouth. Another memory to keep close to her heart.

She let him lead her to the fireplace, where she

stood in front of him. Her hands reached for the ties to her wrapper, which she let puddle at her feet.

A white ribbon wove delicately through the bodice of her silk nightgown. She undid it with a single tug, the barest shimmy sending the material sliding in a whispered caress over her skin, her naked body reflecting the soft glow of firelight.

Rosalyn leaned forward and kissed him, her hands sliding up his soft cotton shirt, her fingers twining in his hair.

He pressed her down on the sofa, his arousal a hard, hot length against her belly, and she moved urgently against him, reveling in the hungry moan that rumbled up his throat and the way his hands tensed against her sides.

Her legs spread around his hips; her pelvis ground against his. His lips swept along her neck, lavishing kisses on every bit of skin, warming her from the inside out, making her tremble with longing.

His lips trailed down the valley between her breasts. Rosalyn bit her lip as Derek's big, warm hand settled on her breast, cupping, massaging, lightly teasing her nipple until it peaked.

Her hand moved instinctively to the waistband of his trousers, sliding provocatively over his erection as his mouth slanted over hers with mounting passion.

Rosalyn felt encompassed in a delirious haze, losing herself more and more with each passing second. Her fingers moved feverishly to undo the buttons on his shirt, then his trousers, both their hands working to free him with haste.

She arched up as his mouth closed over her nipple, her body twisting under his, wanting more.

He manacled both her wrists in one of his hands, holding them above her head as his free hand traveled down her side, gently squeezing her waist, the warmth of his palm settling over her stomach, massaging in slow circles, making her nearly crazy with desire.

She wanted his hands down *there*, his finger slipping between her moist folds. She could feel how ready she was, how wet and throbbing. The tension was almost too much to bear.

She freed one of her hands and gripped his upper arm, her fingers digging into the taut band of muscle, and she lifted up to press a kiss to a small, jagged scar.

He watched her as her lips softly feathered over the injury, her eyes never leaving his as her tongue lightly lapped his skin.

A husky growl traveled up his throat before his mouth came down over hers in a demanding kiss that took her senses away. The heat rising from his body was heady and intoxicating, as a heaviness built at the juncture of her thighs.

He took hold of her hand and moved it up his inner thigh so that her fingers brushed the hardness centered there. Her body quivered as she inched her fingers up, her left hand sweeping against his rigid length. She heard his sharp intake of breath.

He was so virile, so heavenly built. A male in the prime of his life, but with a tempered maturity that made him all the more intoxicating.

She took hold of his erection, massaging him, feeling him swell. Air hissed through his teeth as she cupped him and scratched lightly with her nails.

When she looked up at his face, she saw passion barely in check. He rolled to his back and dragged her across his lap, her naked thighs straddling him. He rocked his erection against her cleft.

He cupped her breasts, and Rosalyn moaned as his thumbs swept across the rigid peaks, making her mindless with desire as he flicked and rubbed and rolled her nipples between his fingers. Her inner lips clenched, a throbbing churning deep inside her.

He tugged her forward, and his tongue flicked a nipple, moistening it, circling, lapping, her body quickening with each passing second.

He moved to her other nipple to lavish it with the same attention before cupping her breasts and pushing them together, drawing one sensitive nub deep into his mouth and then moving to the other to offer it the same attention.

All Rosalyn could do was hold on to his shoulders and pray she didn't faint from pleasure.

The first touch of his finger against her engorged clitoris made Rosalyn buck; the erect tip was hot and exquisitely sensitive, pouring ecstasy through her veins as his mouth created wet paths between her breasts.

She writhed, mindless for that sweet release she knew he could give her, until her back arched, her entire body tensing, lightning gathering deep inside her and spiraling upward as her first convulsion pulsed through her, followed by a second and a third and a fourth as Derek swept a finger inside her, her sheath clutching him with each contraction.

He began to pump, raising her desire once more. She wriggled, wanting him to go deeper, and heard his harsh groan. She ground her hips against him, and he grabbed hold of her wrists, pinioning them at her sides as he stared into her eyes.

With a deep, almost desperate breath, he leaned back and slid into her, her swollen tissue clenching around him as he began to pump, her body sighing into him with each thrust.

He rocked her, his thrusts growing faster, his face racked with an expression that was near to anguish, sweat dampening his brow as he forced himself to slow, slipping out of her entirely in the next moment to massage the nub between her dewy folds with his hot, silky shaft.

Rosalyn cried out with another explosive orgasm, her nails digging into his back as he drove into her again, his hands gripping her buttocks, pulling her tighter against his groin as he plunged deeply.

Suddenly, he snaked his arm behind her back and turned her over so that she was on her hands and knees. He grabbed hold of her hips and slid into her again, her passage wrapping tightly around his shaft as he stroked in and out of her.

He reached his hand beneath her and began massaging her swollen nub, her hair a wild jumble around her face, the long length cascading over her shoulders, her taut nipples peaking through the golden veil each time he pumped.

Mindless, Rosalyn panted his name as he rocked inside her until another shattering release washed over her, and he finally found his own release.

Derek gathered her into his arms and cradled her, his arms wrapped snugly around her waist, their fingers entwined, the fire a soft, warm glow against their skin. In that moment, no wrong existed in the world, and everything that meant anything to her was there on the couch holding her tight.

But reality intruded all too soon. There were things she must tell him, and if she didn't say them now, she might never be able to.

Rosalyn looked into his eyes, and what she saw

made her heart turn over. She loved him. All she knew was that she wanted to be with him—but a daunting hurdle yet remained.

"I can't have children," she told him. "I'm barren. You deserve to know." She closed her eyes. "You deserve a woman who is whole. One who can bear your children."

Derek smiled lovingly. "I *have* a woman who is whole—and she's beautiful, smart, courageous, sensuous, daring, stubborn, and magnificent. Her laugh touches my heart. Her smile feeds my soul. You're the only woman I want, Rosalyn. Did you think I would leave you because of this?"

Rosalyn felt tears brimming in her eyes. "I . . . I didn't know."

Derek held her close. "Why won't you ever let anyone else carry your burdens? You don't always have to be so strong."

"I'm not strong."

Derek tipped her head up. "I don't know another woman who could have faced what you did tonight the way you did. You've been put through hell, yet you never cowered. Please don't do it now. Have faith in me."

Rosalyn smiled tearfully. This man—this beautiful, special man—had been what was missing in her life. She had believed that no man could ever love her and want to marry her.

But someone up above was looking out for her, and she would not let the opportunity pass her by.

It seemed fate was not so fickle, after all.

Love is timeless...

Bestselling historical romance from Pocket Books

One Little Sin
Liz Carlyle

First in an exciting new series!

One sin leads to another...

Two Little Lies
Liz Carlyle
Because just once is never enough!

His Dark Desires
Jennifer St. Giles
Can she resist the passion in his eyes—or
the danger in his kiss?

Outlaw
Lisa Jackson
The only woman who can tempt him is the
one woman he swore to destroy...

The Lawman Said "I Do"
Ana Leigh
All he wanted was a night of pleasure. But
she wanted so much more...

13445

A **love** like you've never known is closer than you think...

Historical Romances from Pocket Books

Can three sisters tame three wild Highlanders? Find out in three sensual stories from bestselling author
Jen Holling

My Wicked Highlander
Her magic is no match for a rugged Scotsman's desire....

My Devilish Scotsman
She doesn't know the strength of her own powers...
or the depth of his desires.

My Shadow Warrior
She desperately needs his help....
He desperately needs her love.

~⁂~

One Night with a Prince
The Royal Brotherhood Series
Sabrina Jeffries
One night of passion....One night of intrigue....
One night with a prince.

Highlander in Love
Julia London
The only thing that separates love and hate...is desire.

12829